THE
CRAIN ADVENTURE

G.D. Crain Jr., circa 1950

THE

CRAIN ADVENTURE

The Making & Building of a Family Publishing Company

Robert Goldsborough

NTC Business Books

a division of *NTC Publishing Group* • Lincolnwood, Illinois USA

Published in conjunction with Crain Communications, Inc.   ᏟᎧ CRAIN BOOKS

Library of Congress Cataloging-in-Publication Data

Goldsborough, Bob.
    The Crain adventure : the making and building of a publishing
giant / Bob Goldsborough.
        p.   cm.
    Includes index.
    ISBN 0-8442-3485-0
    1. Crain Communications Inc.--History. 2. Publishers and
publishing--United States--History--20th century.   I. Title.
Z473.C83G64   1992
381'.45002'0973--dc20   92-7065
                                                          CIP

Published by NTC Business Books, a division of NTC Publishing Group.
4255 West Touhy Avenue
Lincolnwood (Chicago), Illinois 60646-1975, U.S.A.
©1992 by Crain Communications, Inc. All rights reserved.
No part of this book may be reproduced, stored in a retrieval system,
or transmitted in any form by any means,
electronic, mechanical, photocopying, recording or otherwise, without
the prior permission of NTC Publishing Group.
Manufactured in the United States of America.

2 3 4 5 6 7 8 9 ML 9 8 7 6 5 4 3 2 1

This is dedicated to Sid Bernstein, who watched history being made—and who made plenty of history himself along the way.

Foreword

To write a foreword to *The Crain Adventure* is, indeed, an honor. To write it is also a challenge. So much to say. So little space to say it.

My first experience with G.D. Crain, Jr. and his company was in January, 1951 when Bill Marsteller and I opened our little firm. G.D. was our first client. Without him we would have had trouble paying our rent.

G.D. and his great friend, Keith Evans, had been instrumental in founding an industrial advertising association then called the National Industrial Advertising Association (NIAA). It has since become the Business/Professional Advertising Association (B/PAA). My partner Bill Marsteller had been a two-term president of NIAA while he was Vice President of Marketing at Rockwell. He and G.D. became good friends during that period. Thus began a life-long relationship between our two organizations.

We completed a variety of research projects for G.D. as well as writing a series of articles for *Industrial Marketing*, now *Business Marketing*. These early beginnings initiated a warm friendship for us with not only G.D., but with Gertrude Crain and sons Rance and Keith. Both Bill and I benefited greatly from their advice and counsel. And through the years Sid Bernstein, Joe Cappo, Gordon Lewis, Merle Kingman, Jack Graham and many other Crain executives played important roles in the growth of our company.

The wonderful thing about this book is that it not only captures the fascinating history of a great company, but also the entrepreneurial spirit, the publishing innovations, and the risk-taking gambles that characterized a man and his pursuit of journalistic excellence.

It is a book which many people should read. Academic historians, publishing executives, journalism and advertising educators, communications professionals. And students seeking careers in publishing and advertising.

For the Crain Communications employee family, it will not be a "coffee-table" book. It is a living testimony to the spirit of a great journalist, to G.D.'s companion and wife Gertrude, and to Rance and Keith Crain. And the book is a monument also to the hard work and loyalty of dozens of other people who grew fruit in the vineyard of Crain Communications.

Richard C. Christian
Chairman Emeritus, Bursur-Marsteller, Inc.
Associate Dean, Medill School of Journalism
Northwestern University

Acknowledgments

I want to thank the present and past employees of Crain Communications whom I interviewed for the generosity and graciousness with which they gave their time. And I owe a special debt of gratitude to Frances Scott, the company's personnel director, and Mark Mandle, the head librarian, both of whom cheerfully dropped whatever else they were doing on innumerable occasions to help me with a question or a problem.

—R.G.

Contents

❧ PART I ❧

IT ALL BEGAN IN LOUISVILLE

1916–1929

Chapter 1

Kentucky Beginnings

*Don't flip the pages of a periodical and think you
have analyzed the editorial content and the
advertising pull.*

—G.D. Crain Jr.

Like uncounted thousands of American youngsters over the last century, his first job was delivering papers. While being a newspaper car-
rier is the closest most of those masses of youngsters ever get to the
world of the Fourth Estate, Gus Crain, as a teenager, had already
started on a journalistic adventure that was to span more than 70
years.

At the same time he was lobbing copies of the *Times* and the *Herald*
onto porches along the tree-lined streets of his native Louisville, the
young G.D. Crain also was an editor on the newspaper at Louisville
Male High School and had begun to form a vision of his future.

The youth, formally Gustavus Dedman Crain Jr.—he hated his first
name—was born on November 19, 1885, in Lawrenceburg, a small
north-central Kentucky town. He was the second of three sons of
Gustavus Sr. and Annie Edwards Crain. The family, including older
brother Kenneth and younger brother Murray, soon moved to Louisville, where the future publisher attended public schools and began
to hone his writing and editing skills, and to develop his entrepreneurial talents.

"Because money was a very scarce commodity in our family in
those days, I remember with great interest my first efforts as a businessman," he said in an interview decades later. "Knowing that copies
of the afternoon newspapers could be purchased by newsboys for one

cent and resold for two cents, I started my business career with a capital of five cents supplied to me one hot summer morning by my mother. I walked to the office of the *Times,* purchased five copies of the afternoon paper and returned home a couple of hours later with a 100 percent increase in capital.

"I continued this for several weeks and finally found myself with about 25 regular purchasers of the afternoon paper plus a number of others who were buying copies occasionally. This attracted the attention of the circulation department of the *Times,* and I was then given a regular route with compensation on a more even basis, namely $1.50 a week. This continued until I switched to the morning *Herald* because of slightly higher compensation and the fact that it did not interfere directly with high school hours."

While Crain was in high school, one of his English teachers, Ernest Holland, was impressed with his ability and suggested he apply to Indiana University, Holland's alma mater. "However, I had so little money that when I was offered a scholarship to Centre College in Danville, Kentucky, the summer after my high school graduation, I decided to accept." Another reason for the choice, he said, was that because the entrance requirements at Centre were relatively low and his high school records were good, he was able to enter the school as a junior. Altogether, he was at Centre for three years, culminating with a Master's degree in English—a relative rarity in those years. The subject of his thesis was "The influence of German literature on Thomas Carlyle."

Immediately on leaving Centre, Crain joined the staff of the *Louisville Herald,* the same paper he had delivered just a few years earlier. He was taken on as a reporter without a salary and told that compensation would follow only if he showed that he was capable of handling the assignments; after two weeks, he went on the payroll at $10 a week.

Those were adventurous if not always enjoyable days for the young newspaperman. One of his early assignments was to cover the execution of a convicted murderer named William Van Dalsen.

"He was a very pleasant and agreeable chap, and the reporters on the papers, including myself, interviewed him regularly for a few days prior to his hanging. The spectacle unfortunately was regarded as something of a holiday affair by several hundred people who were permitted to crowd into the Jefferson County jail. I remember that the jailer was in tears as he led the convicted man to the gallows.

G.D. Crain Jr. in his student days in Kentucky.

"One of the young reporters who was attending the hanging fainted and collapsed while Van Dalsen's body was suspended from the cross-bar. Later on electrocution was substituted for hanging in Kentucky and the executions at the state penitentiaries were not witnessed by more than the necessary number of legal witnesses, including representatives of the press."

Crain also had the unique experience of scooping the vaunted *Courier-Journal*, the city's largest paper and one of America's most-respected dailies. He covered a speech by the *Courier-Journal*'s flamboyant and legendary owner, Henry Watterson, at a celebration honoring Abraham Lincoln. Watterson discarded his manuscript and launched into an impassioned defense of Nancy Hanks, Lincoln's mother. "The next day," Crain recalled, "our story carried his tribute to Lincoln's mother, while the *Courier-Journal* contented itself with using the prepared manuscript."

Crain looked back on the Louisville of that era as a "hotbed of newspaper talent," in large measure because of the presence of the mighty *Courier-Journal.* Among the major talents in Louisville at that time were Watterson; Arthur Krock, who later became head of *The New York Times* Washington bureau; W.W. Hawkins, who moved from the *Courier-Journal* to United Press and eventually to head of the Scripps-Howard newspaper chain; and artist Fontaine Fox, who would go on to national fame as creator of the "Toonerville Trolley" comic strip.

"During all my work on the *Herald,* which included stints as city editor and sports editor, I was constantly amazed that reporters and editors were paid less than Linotype operators," he said. "I often thought that publishers were short-sighted not to give their staff members adequate compensation, as they constantly lost good men to other fields."

One of the good men the newspaper business eventually lost was Crain himself. In his tenure at the *Herald,* he developed what he modestly termed "some limited knowledge" of business paper activities because, to supplement his income, he served as a correspondent for several business publications, including the *Western Underwriter,* now the *National Underwriter.*

Then as now, the business or "trade" press was a highly segmented industry, with publications, most of them monthlies, covering every conceivable industry, from hardware stores to blast furnaces and from insurance to cigar-making and furniture-making. While many business publications today boast circulations well up into five and even six figures, the trade press of the early twentieth century was rife with periodicals having circulations of under 5,000 and even as low as a few hundred. It was the rare case for a trade magazine to reach the 20,000 plateau.

His work as a correspondent, or "stringer," for business publications whetted Crain's interest. His entrepreneurial juices were flowing, and he sent a form letter to about 600 papers in the trade and industrial fields, offering his services as a news or feature writer. The response was so positive that he left the *Herald* and established a Louisville-based editorial service that produced both news and features for about 100 business publications in a variety of fields, including banking and finance, insurance underwriting, and lumber manufacture and wholesaling.

"One of the men who influenced me in the direction of business publishing was E.H. Defebaugh, who conducted a business in Louisville, publishing several trade journals, including the *Barrel & Box* and *American Stone Trade,*" Crain said. "He later left Louisville and established his company in Chicago, and for a brief period I served as editor of one of those publications."

For his Louisville editorial service Crain assembled a small staff, which "I directed very much as I had reporters in the city room of the *Louisville Herald.* Assignments were given out each morning and the completed copy forwarded that afternoon. While the rates paid were low for the most part," he said, "we were busy covering the news and developing information procedures and consequently turned in a good volume of business."

As invigorating and relatively successful as this editorial service was, however, Crain hungered for something more. "I always wanted to be a publisher," he said in a 1970 interview marking the 40th anniversary of *Advertising Age.* This desire led him to sell his small but healthy business to his employees and, in 1916, at the age of 31, to embark on a career as a publisher—a decision that had a profound effect both on his own life and on the universe of business publishing.

Chapter 2

On to Chicago

Come and show me another city with lifted head
singing so proud to be alive and coarse and strong
and cunning.

—*Carl Sandburg, "Chicago"*

The Chicago that the tall, lanky and studious G.D. Crain found on his arrival in 1916 with his wife and two young daughters was indeed "alive and coarse and strong and cunning," as described by Sandburg in the marquee work of his "Chicago Poems" volume, published that very year. The feisty young metropolis, a hub of transportation, printing, publishing, and food processing, and with a population that had reached two million in the census six years earlier, seemed an ideal place for a young man to seek a publishing career.

Technically, Crain did not begin that career in Chicago, but in his native Louisville, early in 1916. He moved 300 miles north to the Windy City with his wife and daughters a few months later. "My capital consisted of only a few thousand dollars and a great deal of optimism, particularly as I started two publications at almost the same time," he recalled in later years. "My original choice was *Hospital Management*, because I discovered there was only one [other] important publication in the field at that time."

That periodical was *Modern Hospital*, published in St. Louis by Dr. John Hornsby, a former hospital superintendent who also was a consultant on hospital design and equipment. Hospital construction across the U.S. was booming at the time, and Crain felt a magazine devoted to hospital administration would be popular. The first issue of *Hospital Management* appeared in February—36 pages, including 20 pages of advertising. Among the articles in that first-ever Crain peri-

HOSPITAL MANAGEMENT

February, 1916

In This Issue

Announcement of Dates of American Hospital
Association Meeting

• •

Louisville and Cincinnati Organize Hospital
Associations

• •

Nation-Wide Survey of Contagious Hospital
Management

• •

How New York Hospital Gets Efficiency in
Its Laundry

• •

Youngstown Sheet & Tube Company's Model
Industrial Hospital

• •

Record System of Louisville City Hospital

SEE SPECIAL OFFER TO SUBSCRIBERS ON PAGE 5.

Published   Monthly by
CRAIN PUBLISHING CO.
INCORPORATED
LOUISVILLE, KY.

The first-ever Crain publication, *Hospital Management*, made its debut
in February, 1916. The 36-page issue, which included 20 pages of
advertising, went to about 3,000 readers, most of them hospital
administrators.

odical were: reports on the cities of Louisville and Cincinnati organizing hospital associations; how New York Hospital kept its laundry service efficient; Youngstown Sheet & Tube Co.'s "model industrial hospital"; and a nationwide survey of contagion hospital management.

On the editorial page under the heading "Publisher's Announcement," G.D. Crain spelled out the new monthly's mission, saying that it "will be devoted principally to the administration and executive departments of hospital work, and will endeavor to be of practical value to the men and women in charge of the hospitals of the country. To this end we will seek the advice and assistance of all those who are interested in promoting better methods. We shall strive to make *Hospital Management* a forum for the exchange of ideas on every topic of value."

Advertisers in that first issue ranged from makers of toilet paper, sutures, and operating tables to the manufacturer of a new spiral fire escape. It also included Goodwin's Apple Butter ("It is pure, wholesome and delicious and is used in many hospitals") and— incredibly—Old I.W. Harper ("A *safe* whiskey for hospital use").

The 7-by-10-inch magazine went to some 3,000 readers, most of them in positions of hospital administration. The one-time page rate for an ad was $50. Subscriptions were $2 a year.

The issue, Crain said, "got good response from readers, but advertising was slow to develop, partly because promotional facilities were limited. I concluded that a publication devoted to specialized advertising in business publications would interest many manufacturers and advertising agencies which were large users of the specialized business press, and that such a publication would also be a highly effective medium for the promotion of *Hospital Management*."

The result was the debut of *Class* in March. The first issue of the 6¼-by-4¼-inch, digest-sized monthly was 32 pages, with 18 pages of paid advertising. The initial ad rate was $15 a page. Among the charter advertisers were such trade books as *Brick and Clay Record, The Hotel Bulletin, Textile World Journal, The Iron Age, Implement & Tractor Trade Journal,* and *The Inland Printer.* Crain, who was a one-man editorial and advertising department—his staff consisted solely of a secretary—credited his acquaintance with business publications, dating to his days as a correspondent, with the early advertising support for *Class,* terming it "a modest success from the beginning."

Class was so named because in that era business publications fell into three general categories: (1) retail; (2) industrial—publications targeted to specific industries such as railroads, steel and construc-

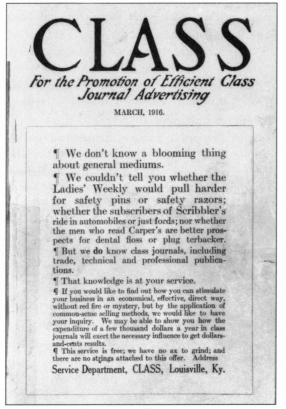

CLASS

For the Promotion of Efficient Class Journal Advertising

MARCH, 1916.

¶ We don't know a blooming thing about general mediums.

¶ We couldn't tell you whether the Ladies' Weekly would pull harder for safety pins or safety razors; whether the subscribers of Scribbler's ride in automobiles or just fords; nor whether the men who read Carper's are better prospects for dental floss or plug terbacker.

¶ But we **do** know class journals, including trade, technical and professional publications.

¶ That knowledge is at your service.

¶ If you would like to find out how you can stimulate your business in an economical, effective, direct way, without red fire or mystery, but by the application of common-sense selling methods, we would like to have your inquiry. We may be able to show you how the expenditure of a few thousand dollars a year in class journals will exert the necessary influence to get dollars-and-cents results.

¶ This service is free; we have no ax to grind; and there are no strings attached to this offer. Address

Service Department, CLASS, Louisville, Ky.

One month after *Hospital Management* appeared, G.D. Crain rolled out his second magazine, *Class*. "I concluded that a publication devoted to specialized advertising in business publications would interest many manufacturers and advertising agencies," he said, adding that *Class* "would also be a highly effective medium for the promotion of *Hospital Management*."

tion; and (3) "class" publications—periodicals aimed at classes of people, that is, those who had the same general functions, regardless of the type of business or industry in which they were employed. Crain's new magazine was targeted primarily at people engaged in business-to-business advertising.

He felt that advertisers "needed to be informed as to how to create effective advertising. We stressed the importance of market research, of which there had been little. We encouraged publishers to feature market information in their advertisements and to offer items of information that would give advertisers a better knowledge of fields they were serving."

The cover of that first issue defined the mission of the publication (see box), proclaiming that "We may be able to show you how the expenditure of a few thousand dollars a year in class journals will exert the necessary influence to get dollars-and-cents results."

From the onset, Crain crusaded for more equitable compensation for agencies handling advertising in business journals; this was the subject of numerous articles in *Class*.

"At the time I started *Class*, business publications didn't allow agency compensations, and very little agency work was done in the field," he said. "Most of the advertisers placed their business direct and relied on publishers for copy service. It wasn't until the '30s that the industrial publications began to pay commissions and to encourage agencies to handle their accounts, because they realized finally that if the copy were better it would produce better results and therefore justify advertisers in making larger expenditures.

"I wasn't campaigning for higher advertising rates just for their own sake, but to enable the publishers to do a better editorial job, a better circulation job, a better job in general. I didn't think most business publishers were providing as complete a service as the advertisers needed. And we felt that with better editorial content and bigger circulations the publishers would earn a higher rate and be able to render a better service."

Crain also was sensitive from the beginning to the potential conflicts between advertising and editorial, which continue today to pose challenges to both business and consumer publications. "In starting my own publications, while in most cases I doubled in brass and handled a good deal of editorial as well as advertising affairs, the editorial objective was to serve the reader—and the advertiser got the benefit in terms of readership that enabled him to tell his sales story effectively. Advertisers generally are looking for publicity, but most of them respect the editorial standards of a publication. . . . If the advertiser knows what the publication wants in the way of editorial content, he very seldom makes an issue of publishing material that has no proper place in the editorial or text pages of the publication.

"I've always regarded myself primarily as an editor and reporter and writer," Crain said. "But I added salesmanship just because I had to. Editorial experience is bound to be helpful in selling, if only . . . that it enables you to give advertisers more information about the field."

It didn't take long after starting up his two publications for Crain to realize that he, like his mentor E.H. Defebaugh, would profit by relocating to Chicago. "I soon discovered that being located in Louisville was a disadvantage, as I found it necessary to go to Chicago and New York on advertising and editorial missions." Consequently, Page 1 of the September, 1916, issue of *Class* carried the following message, under the headline "We've Moved to Chicago": "The offices of *Class* are now in the Windy City...Louisville is one of the best towns on the map (the finest there is, just between us), but as *Class* must be in the center of the trade paper publishing and advertising business, removal to Chicago was a logical step."

The first Crain office in Chicago was on the eighth floor of the Transportation Building at 608 S. Dearborn St., in the heart of the city's "Printer's Row" district just south of the Loop. The Chicago of that day was the indisputable printing capital of the U.S., as well as its trade magazine center. The location was particularly advantageous for *Hospital Management*, with the American Medical Association, the American Hospital Association and the American College of Surgeons all headquartered there.

William "Big Bill" Thompson was serving the first of his three stormy terms as mayor—an era that would be remembered both for the mayor's flamboyance and for rampant graft and corruption in city government. Not all the misdeeds were governmental, however. The "Black Sox" baseball scandal was three years in the future, as was the beginning of Prohibition, which would bring with it Al Capone and the full-blown gangster warfare that the city—to its chagrin—is world-famous for even today.

But Chicago also was a font of unbridled optimism and more than a touch of swagger. It was the nation's rail hub; it boasted the biggest stock yards; its design giants—among them Sullivan, Adler, Wright, and Burnham—were redefining American architecture and engineering. And the Art Institute was in the process of amassing one of the world's great collections of French Impressionist art, thanks in large measure to the city's wealthy merchants and industrialists.

It was an exciting time to be in Chicago, and G.D. Crain relished the stimulation provided by this city on the move. He also realized, however, that putting out two monthlies was a bigger job than one person could handle. "It wasn't until I got to Chicago that I began to appoint representatives and hire salesmen," he said. "As volume increased little by little, I was able to have more time for general planning. In other words, I was really not prepared from the standpoint of either capital or experience to run one publication, much less two,

The Mission of *Class*
From Front Page of First Issue

We don't know the first thing about general mediums.

We couldn't tell you whether the Ladies' Weekly would pull harder for safety pins or safety razors; whether the subscribers of Scribblers ride in automobiles or just Fords; nor whether the men who read Carper's are better prospects for dental floss or plug terbacker.

But we **do** know class journals, including trade, technical and professional publications.

That knowledge is at your service.

If you would like to find out how you can stimulate your business in an economical, effective, direct way, without red fire or mystery, but by the application of common sense selling methods, we would like to have your inquiry. We may be able to show you how the expenditure of a few thousand dollars a year in class journals will exert the necessary influence to get dollars-and-sense results.

This service is free; we have no ax to grind; and there are no strings attached to this offer.

and doing that as well as writing on the side as a means of getting an income for living expenses represented a fairly full schedule."

That "full schedule" of Crain's included frequent trips on both advertising and editorial missions. On one such visit to Washington, after the United States entry into World War I in 1917, he met Herbert Hoover, who had been appointed U.S. Food Administrator and had announced some general regulations affecting food consumption. "I got a statement from him saying that hospitals were not expected to observe the rules and regulations, because the care of the patients came first and therefore they would be able to use foods necessary for proper diet of patients. I played that up big in the next issue of *Hospital Management* and it attracted considerable attention and favorable comment."

Both attention and favorable comment are vitally important to new publications, and G.D. Crain worked hard to garner these for both his publications, making himself and his opinions known to major decision-makers such as Hoover.

For the new publisher, a toehold had been established in the Windy City, and as both a World War and a decade were coming to an end, the future looked rosy indeed.

Chapter 3

Into the Twenties with Gusto

*I would like to acclaim an era of good feeling amid
dependable prosperity and all the blessings which
attend...*
　　—Warren G. Harding, Inaugural Address, 1921

G.D. Crain began the new decade with much of the same boundless
optimism that the country as a whole was feeling. The Great War had
ended in victory, and the U.S. seemed poised to vault into an age of
"dependable prosperity," as the soon-to-be-discredited President
Harding termed it at his inauguration. Indeed, there would be prosperity for many during the "roaring twenties," including Crain and his
fledgling publishing enterprise.

Class, in particular, took off during the heady Postwar years, helped
along by the bullish business climate. By 1923, the year Warren Harding died in office and was replaced by Calvin Coolidge, the young
publication, with a circulation of 5,375 and now charging $45 to $65
a page for advertising, was regularly weighing in at 150-plus pages,
with an occasional 200-page number. Beginning with that year's November issue, the magazine ran Market Data Supplements every
month, covering such categories as automotive and construction industries, hotels and restaurants, and dry goods and clothing. These
sections were created to supply specific and detailed information in
well-defined categories to business-to-business marketers.

The automotive Market Data Supplement in the November, 1923,
Class led off with an article on International Harvester's booming
new business in the manufacture of school buses. And in an unwitting

bit of futurism, a state-by-state listing of the number of registered private automobiles showed that California, with 1,034,000 cars, was easily the leader, although the 1920 census ranked it as only the eighth most-populous state.

As a spinoff of *Class*, in 1921 G.D. Crain began publishing the annual *Crain's Market Data Book and Directory of Class, Trade, and Technical Publications*. Selling for $5, the 1923 edition of this hardbound reference book weighed in at 498 pages. This was the beginning of a company tradition of publishing directories and compendia of information, and marked the first time "Crain" was used in the title of a publication.

By the mid-1920s, *Class* had become *Class & Industrial Advertising* to more accurately reflect its mission. Beginning with the March, 1927 issue, the name was again changed—to *Class & Industrial Marketing*. With this new title, the magazine metamorphasized from digest size to the more standard 8½-by-11 inch magazine format, and handsome color paintings of dramatic industrial settings began to adorn its heavy stock covers.

VOL. XVII   MAY, 1927   No. 7

Employment Record Reveals Wide Seasonal Variations
How Worthington Reaches Man in Overalls
Organizing for Industrial Export Selling

In 1927, the magazine that began as *Class* changed its name to *Class & Industrial Marketing* and grew from digest size to the more standard 8½-by-11-inch magazine format.

Hospital Management also was thriving during these years. By the beginning of the new decade, it had "in the neighborhood of 5,000 paid subscribers," Crain said. "The field was growing, and the circulation continued to increase over the years. We were selling paid subscriptions, although later one or two publications started in the field on a controlled circulation basis. But since there was plenty of paid circulation available, these publications didn't seem to go over too well."

Crain, balancing more than a full plate of work as both editor and publisher of two magazines, hired veteran Chicago newspaper sportswriter Matthew O. Foley to be managing editor of *Hospital Management,* effective with the December, 1920, issue. The masthead for that issue listed G. D. Crain as Editorial Director and his brother, Kenneth C. Crain, as General Manager. Kenneth had moved north in 1919 from Cincinnati, where he had been selling advertising for both publications.

Foley, who "understood the need for public relations," according to G.D. Crain, wasted no time in raising the profile of the magazine. He established National Hospital Day to give hospitals a chance to invite the public to visit them once a year and see their facilities.

"When Matt got this idea, he discussed it with me and asked what I thought would be a suitable day," Crain said years later. "I suggested the birthday of Florence Nightingale, May 12. President Harding issued a proclamation designating that date as National Hospital Day in 1921. We conducted the observance for a number of years and later turned it over to the American Hospital Association for administration."

The magazine—whose editorial content ranged from nuts-and-bolts pieces on hospital design and kitchens and laundries to such prescient articles as one headlined "Should the doctors smoke?"—prospered through the decade, with ad rates by 1923 at $75 to $95 a page. Issues regularly surpassed 80 pages, usually with a 50-50 advertising-editorial ratio.

One of the most important additions ever made to the company occurred in June, 1922. This time it was not a publication but an individual: A 15-year-old high school student from Chicago's South Side, Sidney Bernstein, joined the Crain operation as an office boy during his summer vacation. He was to become its longest-serving employee, rising to the posts of editor and publisher of *Advertising Age.* And on the diamond anniversary of Crain Communications Inc., he continues to play an active role, serving as chairman of the executive committee and writing a weekly column in *Ad Age.*

"I had never heard of Crain, but I answered a newspaper want ad," Bernstein recalled. "I was second choice [as office boy], but the one who got the job only showed up for a day or two, so they hired me."

Bernstein went back to high school and after graduation returned to the Crain job to raise funds so he could attend the University of Illinois in Champaign-Urbana. After a one-year stint at the university ("I ran out of money"), he rejoined the company in 1925 as an assistant editor on *Hospital Management*, reporting to Matt Foley. "He was a wonderful man. He never swore or said anything bad about anyone," said Bernstein, who did his first professional writing for Foley.

It was also in 1922 that the 37-year-old G.D. Crain suffered a tragic loss. His wife, Ailiene Ferris Crain, died, and he was left to rear their two daughters, Jane and Mary. Plunging into his work, he continued to "double in brass" as both editor and publisher of *Class*, although he turned most of the editorial responsibility for *Hospital Management* over to Foley.

He also became active in business and industrial advertising groups, and in the process formed what would be a lifelong friendship with Keith J. Evans, advertising and sales promotion manager of Joseph T. Ryerson & Sons, a Chicago-based steel wholesaler. Crain and Evans were among the founders in the 1920s of the National Industrial Advertisers Association (now the Business/Professional Advertising Association) and Evans became the group's first president.

"One of the things that hadn't been given much attention up to that time was industrial market research," Crain said decades later. "At the NIAA meetings, we began to lay more stress on the importance of getting basic statistical information about industrial markets so that industrial advertisers would have a better picture of the people they were shooting at. The methods discussed seem quite elementary now, but at that time, they were new to many advertisers.

"One of the early addresses at an NIAA conference was made by Al Staehle, then with Westinghouse and later publisher of McGraw-Hill's *Factory*. He described how Westinghouse used information from the Census of Manufacturers to determine their marketing operation, indicating the particular industries that represented the best prospects for electric motors and other Westinghouse equipment. That was a really important development because most industrial advertisers had a very sketchy idea of how they would measure the sales potential of the various markets they were going into."

Crain also recalled an NIAA speech by Bruce Barton, who had recently formed the Barton, Durstine and Osborn advertising agency in

G.D. Crain (back row, second from right) and his lifelong friend Keith Evans (back row, far right) were among the founders of the National Industrial Advertisers Association (now the Business/Professional Advertisers Association). This photo shows members of the newly formed NIAA at an Atlanta meeting in the early 1920s.

New York (later BBDO). "The appearance of Barton fitted right in with what the advertisers were trying to do. They had a considerable inferiority complex and thought their advertising was not regarded as important as general consumer advertising. So they were bringing famous people from the world of general advertising to tell the theory of advertising . . . and to present it in relation to the specific problems of industrial advertising and marketing."

The second half of the 1920s seemed at the time to be a golden age in American history. The stock market was up, up, up. F. Scott Fitzgerald and Ernest Hemingway, two American expatriates living in Paris, burst upon the literary scene. In 1927, Charles A. Lindberg made the first solo airplane flight across the Atlantic, and Babe Ruth of the New York Yankees set a seemingly unreachable record by hitting 60 home runs in a single season. The two Crain publications were ad-heavy and profitable, reflecting the nation's economy as a whole. Amid this prosperity, G.D. Crain was, as he said himself, "looking for new worlds to conquer." And he picked his target.

"I had become familiar with *Printers' Ink* and other advertising journals that were in existence at the time," he said, "and none of them was giving any attention to news developments. For instance, if an advertiser appointed an agency, no mention was made of the previous agency. And if a campaign story was run, the media used were never mentioned. So I decided the field was in need of a news publication and planned to publish a newspaper for advertisers and marketers."

Crain's idea was sound, but his timing could not have been worse. It was late 1929 and, as he enthusiastically laid plans for the launch of his new advertising and marketing publication, an earthquake hit in late October in the form of the stock market crash on Wall Street. The Great Depression had begun.

PART II

THE BIRTH OF A GIANT

1930–1941

Chapter 4

Toughing It Out

These unhappy times call for the building of plans.
—Franklin D. Roosevelt, 1932

Many optimistic plans that were conceived in the bullish, go-go days of the late 1920s got unceremoniously scrapped with the coming of the new decade. But G.D. Crain was not about to let the Depression deter him. Barely 10 weeks after the New York Stock Exchange's "Black Tuesday" debacle of October 29, 1929, his newest brainchild, *Advertising Age*, was launched as a weekly.

"There was no indication at the time that a business depression of long duration was in prospect," Crain recalled. "Most of the forecasts were for a very short recession. At that time, I was president of the National Conference of Business Paper Editors, and we were meeting regularly with President Hoover and his cabinet to discuss business conditions. We were assured by these authorities that prosperity was just around the corner, and that the Depression would not last very long. However, I think I would have gone ahead anyway [with *Advertising Age*], because I had gotten enthusiastic about the idea."

Few outside his own staff shared Crain's enthusiasm when the first 12-page black-and-white tabloid-sized issue, dated January 11, 1930, arrived without fanfare in the offices of advertising people across the country. That premiere issue—*Ad Age* from the beginning has come out on Mondays, with its final editorial deadlines late Friday afternoons—carried stories about the death of long-time *Ladies' Home Journal* editor Edward W. Bok; the winning of a five-day work week by printers and engravers; how Pepsodent Co. and Quaker Oats

Less than three months after the "Black Tuesday" stock market crash in 1929, the 12-page maiden issue of *Advertising Age* arrived without fanfare on the desks of some 10,000 advertising people across the United States. Advertising for that first edition was barely more than anemic, reflecting both skepticism about the new weekly and concern about the Depression economy.

were sole sponsors of daily radio programs—Pepsodent's being the immensely popular "Amos n' Andy"; and General Motors being the leading 1929 advertiser with expenditures of more than $8 million.

"Rough Proofs," a column of brief items, signed by "Copy Cub," (a G.D. Crain *nom de plume*) ran down the left side of Page One. Written by Crain, it would continue to be a staple of *Ad Age* for 35 years. Among the "Rough Proofs" in that first issue:

> "The publisher who tried to popularize a bridge magazine went into bankruptcy. Evidently, he failed to make his contract.

> "*The New Yorker* says that mornings are a burden to humanity and should be abolished. The chap who wrote that had probably just finished reading the bright and cheery alarm clock advertisements which tell how to roll out smilingly at 6 a.m.

> "The new Ruxton [automobile] announces that included in its line is a saloon for five passengers. The details are not given, but of course a brass rail and a sawdust box are among the appointments.

> "*Printers' Ink* recently reported that a new publication was being started 'at' Chicago. It's permissible to say 'at' Horse Cave, Ky., or 'at' Kennebunkport, Me., but in referring to New York and Chicago, *P.I.*, let's say 'in.' "

Advertising support for that premiere issue was barely more than anemic. The 11 charter advertisers included the *Washington Post, Seed World, Broadcast Advertising, Boot & Shoe Recorder, Golfdom, National Dry Goods Reporter, Playgoer,* and a publication titled *The New Era in Food Distribution*, which took out the only full-page ad in the issue.

"No hoopla of any kind—not even a modest prior announcement—welcomed *Advertising Age*," Sid Bernstein wrote on the 60th anniversary of the publication in 1990. "It just appeared on the desks of 10,000 people, heralded by a modest, two-column front-page announcement, 'Why We Are Here' " (see box). That first issue was sent free to names culled from the Standard Advertising Register, although the weekly paper was listed on page one as costing "Three Cents a Copy—$1 a Year."

"Outside reaction came quickly, most of it not favorable," continued Bernstein, who at the time of the startup was still an associate editor of *Hospital Management,* although within three years he would be *Ad Age's* managing editor. "In fact, the general reaction, especially among friends, was that Mr. Crain's business judgment was subject to serious question."

Among the comments from critics that Bernstein catalogued: "Why do we need another advertising paper?" "A general advertising paper to be published in Chicago? All advertising papers are published in New York, logically; that's where the business is." "Does he expect to go head-to-head against *Printers' Ink* . . . one of the leading business papers in the world?"

G.D. Crain did indeed expect to battle straight up against the powerful and well-entrenched *Printers' Ink.* His background as a newspaperman had imbued him with a keen news sense that was to shape and distinguish his publications and pervade their coverage. He was among the first business journalists to recognize the necessity of quickly and accurately informing his readers of outside events and actions affecting them—such as federal, state and local regulation, and the activities and influence of pressure groups.

In its particular sphere, *Advertising Age* was really entering virgin territory, as no publication except *Printers' Ink* was covering the industry in any way. Crain pointed out years later that in 1930 there were no newspaper advertising columns and no regional publications reporting on the field.

"We began to report account changes and indicate the previous agencies and in some cases the reasons for the change of accounts. We were also reporting campaign stories in detail, giving the lists of media used, particularly where changes in media policy were involved."

The media was an important part of *Ad Age's* constituency. As current editor Fred Danzig wrote in the 60th anniversary issue, "By triangulating the advertising universe, G.D. believed *Ad Age* would become an essential, powerful business force. He saw it cultivating sources among advertisers (the buyers), media (the sellers), and agencies (the buyers and sellers) on the strength of its information-packed news columns."

Ad Age had no full-time reporters at the beginning. G.D. Crain was writing editorials and some of the stories from the Chicago office. His brother Murray, also in Chicago, was a managing editor without a staff, and the paper had one editorial person based in New York.

Much of *Ad Age's* coverage in its first years centered on government regulations. "We were afraid that legislation giving increased power to the Federal Trade Commission would hamper advertising and marketing severely," Crain said, "so we were constantly urging advertising organizations and the agency people and the publishers to emphasize self-regulation to eliminate the abuses of advertising, so that government regulation wouldn't be necessary."

The first three years were tough ones for the young publication as the country slid deeper into the worst economic trough in its history. G.D. Crain once again doubled in brass, dividing his time between writing and editing on the one hand and selling advertising and drumming up enthusiasm for the paper on the other—although the word wouldn't be coined for at least 30 years, Crain was truly a "workaholic." Sid Bernstein remembers that during those years, the Crain offices were moved from the third to the thirteenth floor of 537 S. Dearborn St. across the street from the building in Printer's Row that had been the company's first Chicago home. "Everybody was running around carrying boxes and cartons, and through all the noise and confusion, G.D. sat at his typewriter, oblivious to it all, pounding out copy."

But Bernstein also fondly remembers their lunches in those early days. "He and I and perhaps another staffer would jog (and I do mean jog) down two blocks to Dearborn Station, where the Santa Fe Railway would frequently disgorge Hollywood celebrities and where the famed Fred Harvey organization maintained a fine restaurant. G.D. was very much interested in sports, especially baseball, so the Cubs, Sox, and other baseball entities were likely to get an extensive airing. But anything from politics to business was free to occupy eating time in the perfectly free atmosphere of fellows enjoying relaxation at lunch."

Crain's boundless enthusiasm helped carry him through the darkest days of the Depression. "He was perennially optimistic," Bernstein recalls, "the kind of guy not at all overwhelmed because he didn't have much money. As long as there was enough to live on, he was all right."

His drum-beating and selling efforts for *Advertising Age* were frustrated from the start, however, by the economic realities of the day. In a short time he had gone from being the owner of two profitable business publications to presiding over three that were hemorrhaging money. By July, 1933, things were so bad that *Class & Industrial Marketing* was merged into the weekly *Ad Age*, becoming the younger publication's second section on the first Monday of every month as a cost-cutting device. *Class,* which adopted *Ad Age's* overall format and

Class & Industrial Marketing
section of
Advertising Age

Advertising Age published weekly. This section published with first issue of month.

JANUARY 6, 1934   In Two Parts—Part 2   5 C

As the Depression wore on, all three Crain publications were losing money. As a cost-cutting maneuver in July, 1933, *Class & Industrial Marketing* was merged into *Advertising Age*, becoming the weekly's second section on the first Monday of each month. This arrangement continued until 1935, when *Industrial Marketing* (the word *Class* had been dropped from the title) became a free-standing magazine once again.

appearance, generally was a 12-page section during this period, with about five pages of advertising, while *Ad Age* was normally in the 20–32-page range.

Ever the optimist, Crain made even this drastic austerity move sound like a step ahead. The two-page consolidation announcement that ran in the June, 1933, issue of *Class & Industrial Marketing* was headlined "Expanded Service for Readers and Advertisers." Body copy described the move as "the most important improvement we have ever been able to offer" and stressed that *C&IM* advertisers "will have the benefit of the rapidly growing circulation of *Advertising Age*, which is now the most popular advertising publication in the country."

There was at least one bright spot during these gray years: A rock of the Crain organization was Ellen Kebby, who had joined the company in 1921 and was in charge of the office work and the accounting. The English-born Ms. Kebby had, in the words of Sid Bernstein, "a remarkable ability to keep bill collectors pacified." G.D. Crain concurred: "Apparently without telling me, she kept our credit in reasonably good shape. I was never bothered by people who wanted to know when they were going to be paid, and so I was always convinced because of the response from readers—and also the indication of ultimate response from advertisers—that *Advertising Age* was going to be a success."

Why We Are Here

Advertising Age, the National Newspaper of Advertising, has been developed to meet a definite need.

Presenting the news of advertising—a business of widespread interests and ramifications, involving expenditures of two billion dollars a year—has never been the primary, exclusive function of any advertising publication.

That is the task to which *Advertising Age* will devote itself. Each week in these columns will be found the record of events in the world of advertising; the news of advertisers, of agencies, of publications and other mediums; and the news of general developments which affect marketing and hence advertising.

With an organization that has had fourteen years of successful publishing experience, with a staff familiar with the activities and personnel of the advertising and publishing fields, with a group of news-gatherers covering not only the chief centers of advertising, but the whole country, *Advertising Age,* the National Newspaper of Advertising, is ready to function.

We hope to merit the appreciation and good-will of our readers and advertisers.

His continuing enthusiasm helped sustain G.D. Crain through those dismal days. From a perspective of four decades, he reminisced: "I remember on one occasion [during the Depression] I was calling on Walter N. Lamb, who was advertising manager of the *Minneapolis Tribune*. He let me tell my complete story, and when I got all through he leaned back and laughed and said, 'You really believe this stuff, don't you?' I said, 'Yes, I do, I think it's great.' He said, 'Well, I can't give you any business right now, but I promise you as soon as we start promoting again you'll be on the list.' And we were."

Showing himself to be ever the optimist, Crain even saw the benefit of beginning an enterprise in the midst of international economic disarray. "If we had started under more favorable conditions, it's quite possible other people would have been able to establish a publication with much better facilities than we were able to muster with our limited resources. But we worked it out, adding to our staff as revenues grew, so little by little we built up a successful operation. It took a lot of time and effort."

Ironically, the size of G.D. Crain's young publishing operation—only a handful of employees, including himself and his two brothers—worked in its favor during the Depression. There was no fat to pare from the payroll or from the overhead, no wrenching changes such as those that bedeviled other companies in the grim days of the early 1930s when the world seemed to be collapsing.

Chapter 5

Better Days

*In 1934, we began to pick up considerable
business because we had won a reputation for news
reporting and had attracted a lot of readers.*
　　　　　　　　　　　　　　　—*G.D. Crain Jr.*

The above quote referred to *Advertising Age*, but it could be applied
to the rest of G.D. Crain's small company, too. As the 1930s wore on, it
appeared the worst of the Depression was past. Times had been particularly hard in the first three years of the decade, with ad linage cut
drastically and all three Crain publications bathed in red ink.

Sid Bernstein remembers those lean years, not necessarily with
nostalgia: "I got married in 1930. My wife was making $25 a week, I
was getting $50; then she lost her job and I took a 10% pay cut. We
went from $75 a week to $45. But we were lucky—I did have a job.
You didn't spend an extra nickel in those days.

"I recall the day in 1933 when Matt Foley got a call from his
brother, Joe, the sports editor of the *Chicago Journal*, with some wonderful news," Bernstein said. "Joe had run a boxing tourney for the
paper the night before. The tourney ended late, long after the bank
had closed, so Joe took the $11,000 in receipts and put them in a
safety deposit box on the second floor of a building at the corner of
State and Madison Streets—the busiest intersection in Chicago. The
next day, Roosevelt declared the 'bank holiday' shuttering all the
banks [and at least temporarily freezing everyone's accounts]. Joe's
news was that if Matt needed money, it was there for him."

Even better news, from G.D. Crain's standpoint, was that one of his
publications, *Ad Age*, began turning a modest profit in 1934 as the

overall economy improved. "We added staff and facilities and began to do the kind of news reporting job that I realized was needed, but which we couldn't do earlier because of lack of funds," he said.

That year also saw *Ad Age's* first major editorial project—a special section commemorating the 20th anniversary of the Audit Bureau of Circulations, which certifies the circulations of newspapers and magazines. The section, Part 2 of the October 13 issue, was 16 pages, about five of which were paid advertising.

Ad Age's lead editorial that week also praised the ABC: "It hardly seems likely that advertising would have developed so fast and have reached such large volume if the ABC had not been operating. . . . Advertising has been used in generous measure as an economical form of business promotion because business executives have been impressed with the fact that they could buy advertising with full information as to what they were purchasing, in terms of circulation."

Another, less momentous item in the same issue underscored how social mores and popular culture have changed since the 1930s. It was a two-column picture of a new print advertisement for Camel cigarettes. The ad, which broke just after the St. Louis Cardinals defeated the Detroit Tigers in the '34 World Series, was fashioned in the manner of a newspaper front page, with the banner headline: "21 OUT OF 23 ST. LOUIS CARDINALS SMOKE CAMELS." The "lead" story in the ad was bylined by Cardinals' player-manager Frankie Frisch, who extolled the fact that all but two of his champions used the brand.

One significant barometer of the generally improving economy in 1934 was the overall increase in magazine advertising linage. *Ad Age*, which now carried the eagle symbol of the Roosevelt-created National Recovery Administration (NRA) on its nameplate, reported in its December 15 issue that most major magazine categories showed double-digit increases in November over the same month in 1933. Women's magazines were up 14.7%, outdoor magazines (hunting, fishing, etc.), 22.2%, and the weeklies and bi-weeklies, (every other week), 14.5%. Although the Depression was to hang on until the onset of World War II, the worst was over.

The next year, the climate had improved to the point where G.D. Crain felt ready to cut *Class & Industrial Marketing* loose from *Ad Age*, to which it had been tethered for two years. Beginning with the June, 1935, issue, it was a free-standing magazine once more, although *Class* was dropped from the title (the term "class" publications had fallen from usage). In a spread ad on pages 4 and 5 of that issue, trade publication powerhouse McGraw-Hill hailed the return of the magazine. Following is a portion of the text:

"One of the heartening signs of this Nation's recovery from the depths of economic depression is the willingness of business-men to undertake new enterprises. For this, and other reasons, McGraw-Hill welcomes *Industrial Marketing*, which, with this issue, takes its place as an independent publication under the direction of G.D. Crain Jr.

"McGraw-Hill welcomes *Industrial Marketing* because advertising and selling to industry is a big industry in itself and there is obviously a real need for a well-informed, vigorous publication in this particular field."

An editorial in the same issue trumpeted the rebirth: "We believe that in the magazine we have planned for continued promotion and discussion of sound marketing policies in the industrial field, we shall have ample opportunities to play a part in the marked development of these activities now underway."

It also was in 1935 that the Crain offices moved a mile north from their longtime Printer's Row location to the third floor of an all-but-empty building at 100 E. Ohio St., just off Michigan Avenue. At the time of the move, the only other tenant of the six-story white terra cotta building was the Gossard Corset Co. This area north of the Chicago River was beginning to flourish as an upscale retailing district and home to many of the city's large advertising agencies, making it a logical base of operations for *Ad Age*.

In March, 1936, *Business Marketing* celebrated its—and the company's—20th anniversary. The reborn magazine's lead editorial marked the milestone: "The coordination of all marketing functions with the establishment of a definite and centralized method of control has been the outstanding objective of intelligent effort in the industrial field during the last 20 years. In this effort, we believe *Industrial Marketing* has played some part."

G.D. Crain was unable to compose a similar anniversary message in *Hospital Management*, however. The year before, in January, 1935, its longtime editor and conscience, Matt Foley, died of a heart attack at the age of 44. Less than six months later, Crain sold the monthly to Institutional Publications Inc. of Chicago. "He'd lost interest in it," Sid Bernstein said of *Hospital Management,* "and Matt's death had a great deal to do with that. Matt was the heart of the magazine."

Hospital Management was gone—at least for the moment—but both *Ad Age* and *Industrial Marketing* were beginning to thrive along with the economy in general. Despite the untimely loss of a valued colleague, times were good for G.D. Crain, and they were about to get even better.

On a 1936 trip to New York, he called on a vice president of the National Broadcasting Company in NBC's Rockefeller Center headquarters. Whatever the business reason for his visit, it was rendered insignificant because of what transpired. Crain was ushered into the VP's office by his secretary, a New York native named Gertrude Ramsay. That first meeting was literally electric.

She recalled that "As I went to the office to let him in, he turned the knob on his side, and a spark flew. I was embarrassed, he was embarrassed, and we laughed about it." A few minutes later, her boss summoned her into the office. "I don't know why, but this man would like to meet you personally," he told her, gesturing toward Crain.

"He wanted to know if I'd have dinner with him, and I kept telling him no," she said of that first meeting. "Every time he came to town, he'd ask me, and I'd say no, because I really knew nothing about him. Finally I broke down, and we had lunch."

That was the beginning of an accelerated courtship that culminated later in 1936 with the marriage of G.D. Crain and Gertrude Ramsay. A new chapter was about to begin.

Chapter 6

The Calm Before the Storm

I assume the solemn obligation of leading the
American people forward along the road over
which they have chosen to advance.
　　　　—Franklin D. Roosevelt, Second Inaugural,
　　　　　　　　　　　　　　January 20, 1937

Brave words from the recently reelected president, in the midst of a Depression. But as 1937 began, there was a general feeling of optimism across the country, a feeling reflected by *Ad Age* in an editorial on January 11: "With 1937 under way, it is evident that [American industry's] use of advertising will be upon a larger scale than for a long time." In fact, however, there was to be a sharp business downturn the next year, but G.D. Crain was optimistic as 1937 began.

"He was feeling more confident by then," Gertrude Crain said of her husband. "In the early years, obviously it was a toss-up [as to whether *Ad Age* would survive]. Now business was good and things started turning around." Indeed, the weekly's ad volume in 1936 hit 1,500 pages, up from 932 in 1934, and paid circulation surpassed 12,000, an increase of more than 3,000 in two years.

One event buoying Crain's confidence was a ringing affirmation of his publishing acumen. "We got a great boost in 1937 when [advertising agency] BBDO made a readership study among the principal national advertising executives on behalf of one of its clients to determine which publications had the best coverage," he said years later. "This was the first readership study in which *AA* finished first, and of course news of this result helped attract considerable new business."

Among the new business joining the pages of *AA* on a regular basis was advertising for two publications introduced within weeks of each other—magazines that would forever alter the medium. *Life*, a pictorial weekly brought out by *Time* magazine co-founder Henry R. Luce, debuted in December, 1936. Two months later, the Des Moines-based Cowles family's *Look* entered the field as "the Monthly Picture Magazine" (it would later increase its frequency to every other week).

In a pre-publication ad in the January 4, 1937, issue of *AA*, Gardner Cowles Jr. and John Cowles trumpeted their soon-to-be-born baby with an unusual approach: "*Look* is not a magazine designed to impress prospective advertisers. Don't look for coated paper or fancy printing in *Look*. Do look for reader interest, for yourself, for your wife, for your secretary, for your office boy. . . . When you read *Look*, please remember that once, and not so many years ago, *Time, The New York News* and *The Reader's Digest* also were experiments—as is *Look*."

Although *Ad Age* was now firmly established, the business downturn that hit in 1938 did not spare the eight-year-old weekly. Ad volume plummeted some 600 pages from the previous year's level.

And in an ironic twist, G.D. Crain found himself once again at the helm of three publications in 1938; *Hospital Management* was back in the fold. "We couldn't make it," Marshall Reinig said in a 1991 interview of his short-lived ownership of *HM*. He and Francis Shondell had left Gillette Publishing Co. (now Scranton-Gillette Communications Inc.) to start Institutional Publications Inc. in 1935 and buy *HM* from Crain. "The field got overcrowded and we had to give up the ghost. We went broke," Reinig said. "We canceled out our [financial] obligation by returning the magazine to Crain."

As Sid Bernstein recalls, the return of *Hospital Management* after a three-year absence was not greeted with glee by Crain, who had his hands full keeping his other two titles afloat in the rough and unpredictable seas of the post-Depression recession. But he was not about to let this uninvited returnee sink, and he supported *HM* sufficiently so that when the magazine was sold for good more than a decade and a global war later, it was in the black.

The year 1939 brought both the good news of economic recovery after the '38 dip and the bad news of war in Europe. After a series of preliminary turmoils—Italy's invasion of Ethiopia in 1935; the Spanish Civil War's onset in 1936; Japan's attack on China in 1937; and Hitler's Germany muscling its way into Austria and Czechoslovakia in

1938—World War II began on September 1 with the German invasion of Poland.

Although American entry into the war would not come for more than two years, the Crain publications during this period were filled with articles about the impact of the European war on U.S. business in general and marketing and advertising in particular. Voicing a widespread sentiment, *Ad Age*, in an editorial that ran shortly after Hitler's armies entered Poland, said that "America does not want war, nor yearn for war profits." Whatever the country's yearnings, however, the economy recovered mightily at decade's end, and this recovery was shared by *Ad Age* and *Industrial Marketing*, both of which showed renewed advertising vigor.

IM, which in 1939 occasionally exceeded 80 pages per issue, broke the 100-page mark several times in 1940. More significantly, the magazine was firmly establishing itself as a dynamic advocate and defender of business-to-business advertising. In 1936, it had begun the "Copy Chasers" feature that continues today.

In introducing this analysis and critique of specific business advertisements, which began with the title "O.K. As Inserted" (the column was signed simply "Copy Chasers"), *IM* argued that, "So far there has been no one to pass the bouquets to the *industrial copywriter.* Successful industrial campaigns come and go—and credit for them seldom gets any further than the logo at the bottom of the page. Yet behind the scenes, there must be a copy man, or idea man . . . who dreams and frets—who thinks and swears—who writes and rewrites—those successful campaigns and noteworthy advertisements. So—in order that the best of his race go not unnoticed, the intention of this feature is to cull from the hundred-odd trade and technical magazines the best examples (in our opinion) of industrial selling-in-print, and bring them to your attention."

An editor's note with that initial column stated that, "Selection of the advertisements and the comments about them in this article are those of a publisher's representative and an agency executive, both active in organized industrial advertising work." It was only later that Howard "Scotty" Sawyer of the Marsteller ad agency emerged publicly as the "Copy Chaser."

Although G.D. Crain had been the *de facto* editor of *Ad Age* since its birth, his titles were president and publisher, and the highest editorial rank had been that of managing editor, held by several individuals in the publication's first decade. That changed in 1940. In the

February 5 issue, a three-paragraph item on staff changes on Page 2 opened with the announcement that "S.R. Bernstein, formerly director of research and promotion, has been named editor of *Advertising Age* and Irwin Robinson, managing editor, who has been operating in Chicago, will hereafter be headquartered in New York."

Even with a new editor in harness, the publisher continued to maintain a high profile and dispense advice. In a speech to the Advertising Club of Omaha in December, 1941, G.D. Crain urged advertisers to counter attacks against their business and defend themselves aggressively by telling the public about the benefits of advertising.

"We have got to start using the successful political technique of talking to people in their own language and in terms of their own interests. We want to fight for the free competitive system of enterprise which has made America great, but it must be translated to the individual in terms of a better job, greater security of employment, better products and lower prices...

"First of all, every businessman and especially every advertiser should know the consumer and work with consumer groups... Meet with women's clubs, parent-teacher associations and other consumer organizations, and tell them how manufacturers and merchants are supplying more product information through new methods of labeling."

Crain concluded by saying that "the solution is not to hold meetings of advertising men and condemn those who have attacked our business institutions, but to carry the message to Garcia by convincing every part of the public that business in America exists to serve, and that advertising is the voice of service."

That ringing defense of the advertising industry came just five days before Japanese aircraft droned across the Pacific and dropped thousands of tons of explosives on the U.S. military installations at Pearl Harbor, Hickam Field and Schofield Barracks in Hawaii, bringing the U.S. into the war on December 7, 1941, which President Franklin D. Roosevelt termed "a date which will live in infamy."

Advertising now had a new task, as outlined in an *Ad Age* editorial on December 15:

"Because we have been thinking in terms of the participation of the United States in the world struggle, and have been preparing for it for a long time, the period of adjustment to the new situation will be short. Business will settle down to the hard job ahead with concentration and determination, and advertising will be called on to perform its primary role of keeping the public informed of everything it should know about what industry is doing for the national welfare."

PART III

WAR, RECOVERY AND BOOM

1941–1965

Chapter 7

A Nation at War

*There are many essential services which advertising
is called upon to perform in wartime.*

—G.D. Crain Jr.

The above quote was used in a speech G.D. Crain gave to the Cleveland Advertising Club on January 23, 1942, barely six weeks after American entry into World War II. In this talk, he also set forth what he saw as six objectives for wartime advertising:

1. Speed governmental accomplishment in the drive for victory.

2. Expedite conversion of industry to wartime production.

3. Ease the shock of war on civilian population and national economy.

4. Divert demand from scarce articles to those more plentiful.

5. Explain business to the public.

6. Condition markets for postwar developments.

Throughout the nearly four years of U.S. participation in the conflict, Crain kept his publications strongly focused on the myriad ways that marketing and advertising could aid the war effort. For instance, in a January, 1944, editorial, *Industrial Marketing* urged the conservation of paper by advertisers and publications, listing five general ways this could be effected:

"(1) Getting the most out of each sheet of paper; (2) using the lightest practical weights and the more readily available papers; (3) using smaller sizes or changing formats; (4) reducing spoilage and waste; (5) eliminating waste in inventories and in distributions of printed material."

Under paper rationing guidelines set down by the War Production Board, the Crain publications, like most others, were limited to 75% of the prewar annual consumption. "[This] meant we couldn't in-

During World War II, *Advertising Age*, like other publications, lived with the rationing of paper. "One year during the war, we had to turn down 600 pages of advertising," said G.D. Crain.

crease our volume," Crain said. "But because many advertisers who were engaged in war production continued to advertise for public relations purposes, and most media were still getting a considerable volume of business, we had more advertising offered to us that we could carry with our limited paper supply. One year during the war we had to turn down 600 pages of advertising."

Ad Age circulation, which had been 13,000 when the war began, dropped to 11,700 in 1942 before slowly rising to its prewar level before the end of the fighting. During the war, Crain started a monthly publication for servicemen that summarized advertising news. "We sent copies to advertisers and others who asked for them so they in turn could mail them to their servicemen overseas," he said. "In addition, we put out a weekly 'highlight edition' of *Advertising Age* for people whose subscriptions were held up because of the paper shortage."

In 1939, *Ad Age* had established a Washington bureau to more closely monitor government involvement in and regulation of advertising by covering the activities of such agencies as the Federal Trade Commission and the Federal Drug Administration. The first chief of the bureau was A.P. "Bart" Mills, who was succeeded by Hal Burnett and then John Crichton. When Crichton joined the Navy in 1943, he was replaced by Stanley E. Cohen, a recent graduate of Cornell and Columbia Universities, who at the time of his hiring was a reporter for *Broadcasting* magazine.

Stan Cohen, who was to remain the head of *Ad Age's* Washington bureau for more than 40 years, recalled that the link between his one-man operation and the Chicago headquarters during his first years on the job would seem primitive by today's standards. "Most of our communications were by Western Union telegram," he said. "It was difficult—and expensive—in those days to make long distance calls. Plus there were war priorities on use of the phone lines. When I didn't use Western Union, I mailed stories to Chicago that were typed on the backs of Western Union sheets. I didn't like their letterhead at the top, so I used the backs. I was such a tightwad that I never bought any paper."

Both personally and professionally, there was more to the Crain world in the first half of the 1940s than the war in Europe and the Pacific. G.D. and Gertrude were busy rearing two sons, Rance, born in 1938, and Keith, born in 1941 and named after his father's longtime friend and colleague, Keith Evans.

Gertrude Crain remembers fondly her husband's love of baseball—both the big league and the sandlot variety—and how he transmitted that love to his sons during their school years in suburban Evanston. "In the warm-weather months, he would come home from the office, take off his jacket, and go with the boys to the neighborhood baseball diamond," she said. "Before you knew it, he had a couple of teams of children tagging along behind him. He was like a Pied Piper. And this happened every night!"

In 1943, the company, then known as Advertising Publications Inc., became a pioneer in instituting an employee profit-sharing plan. The

Throughout World War II, the Crain publications strongly supported the War Bonds campaign, and as the outcome of the conflict became apparent, they urged readers to begin planning for a postwar economy.

plan, which remains in effect today, always has been totally funded by the company.

Also in 1943, *Advertising Age* made a minor but significant alteration in its subtitle—from "The National Newspaper of Advertising" to "The National Newspaper of Marketing." This shift signaled the forward-looking recognition by Crain and his staff that the 13-year-old publication had as its universe not just advertising, but every phase of the marketing mix.

An editorial on January 11, 1943, announcing the change said in part that "…in discussing the interests and activities of advertisers, *Advertising Age* has studied and reported developments in market research, in distribution, in sales and sales promotion, in packaging, in store and window displays, and in fact has dealt with everything which is part of a successful merchandising operation. Advertising is the expression and vehicle for that type of marketing effort, and to understand the purposes and objectives of advertising, it is necessary to understand marketing in its broadest aspects."

In the last phases of the war, when it became apparent that the Allies would be victorious, both *Advertising Age* and *Industrial Marketing* consistently urged their readers to begin planning for a Postwar economy—which had in essence been Point 6 of G.D. Crain's 1942 speech to the Cleveland Ad Club. And when peace finally came in 1945, *Ad Age* welcomed it with a page one editorial on August 20, written by Sid Bernstein and titled "Now It's Up to Us":

> "…neither military men nor production men can win the peace. The magnificent productive capacity of American industry…must be utilized now for the rehabilitation of a devastated world, for the constant improvement of standards of living, for the fulfillment of human wants and the creation of a solid economic foundation on which all hope of peace eventually rests. This is a job for the marketing man—for the merchandiser, the salesman, the advertiser…. The 'postwar' world—the world we are living in *now*—is the marketing man's oyster. We are confident of his ability to crack it."

Chapter 8

The Postwar World

*Sixteen hours ago, an American airplane dropped
one bomb on Hiroshima.*
                    —*Harry S. Truman, Aug. 6, 1945*

It is difficult for anyone not present then to fully comprehend the initial euphoria with which the war's end was greeted. After Japan's surrender in August, 1945, following the dropping of devastating nuclear bombs on Hiroshima and Nagasaki which ushered in the atomic age, revelries went on around the clock in big cities and hamlets from coast to coast. An estimated two million people flocked to New York's Times Square, and in Los Angeles, celebrants commandeered street cars, leaping from the roof of one trolley to the next.

After the early glow wore off and the troops returned home by the tens of thousands, problems began to emerge—rampant inflation, food shortages, housing shortages, nationwide coal and rail strikes. All this was not enough to put the brakes on the economy, however. The desire for consumer goods was intense following the years in which manufacturing had been geared almost totally toward the war effort. The American productive machine shifted into high gear to feed this insatiable hunger for goods, which included nylon stockings, the early television sets with their 12-inch screens, and the first automobiles to roll off the assembly lines in four years, among them models from Kaiser-Frazer, the first new company to produce American cars in more than 20 years.

New products meant fresh advertising and promotion, and more of it, along with an expansion of roles for the business. In *Ad Age's* first

1946 editorial, January 7, Sid Bernstein wrote that "Advertising has emerged from the war with a new stature, new tasks and new duties. It will never again be confined only to the sale of goods and services. It has too clearly demonstrated its potency in the promulgation of ideas to be overlooked in the struggle of social concepts."

One interesting "social concept" sidelight that is as current in the 1990s: *Ad Age* reported on January 14, 1946, that in a controversial campaign, Seagram Distillers Corp. was saluting moderation in ads for "The Lost Weekend," a film starring Ray Milland that was based on Charles Jackson's 1944 novel about an alcoholic. Some elements within the liquor industry were violently opposed to the campaign, *Ad Age* said, while others regarded it as a "courageous and enlightened" example of public relations.

Advertising in *Ad Age* continued to be heavily weighted toward the media, particularly newspapers. In the late 1940s, the country had not yet fully entered the era of failing big-city papers and one-paper markets, and most major metropolitan areas had at least three dailies, with some—New York, Boston and Chicago among them—boasting five or more. This led to heated competitive newspaper advertising in the trade press, with *Ad Age* in particular a beneficiary.

One new non-print-media advertiser in the pages of *AA* was the American Broadcasting Co., which until 1943 had been part of the National Broadcasting Co. as NBC Radio's "Blue Network." In commenting on *Ad Age's* rapid advertising growth in the Postwar period, G.D. Crain singled out the broadcasters, "who we had not sold successfully to any great extent prior to the war [but who] became much more active and aggressive advertisers after 1945 and 1946."

There was a new broadcast medium looming that would alter forever the society and the culture. Television rapidly and pervasively injected itself into the collective American consciousness—as an advertising medium, an entertainment vehicle and a news source. *Ad Age* aggressively covered the phenomenon, including such early stars as Milton Berle of "The Texaco Star Theatre," Sid Ceasar and Imogene Coca of "Your Show of Shows" and Ed Sullivan with his Sunday night variety show.

In 1949, one million U.S. households had TVs; that number increased tenfold in just two years, and within five years, more than half the homes in the country had at least one set, probably with a "rabbit ears" antenna on top. In September, 1951, a coast-to-coast coaxial cable link enabled the entire country to see TV programs simultaneously.

Radio was being eclipsed, although it didn't give up its premiere broadcast position without a fight. And many advertisers were cautious in embracing the new medium. In 1950, Procter & Gamble, the country's—and radio's—largest advertiser, indicated continued support for radio. *Ad Age* quoted Howard Morgens, P&G's vice president for advertising (and later chairman) as saying that the company was in "no rush to give up radio properties" and that "at best, we believe television as an advertising medium has a bumpy, uneven road before it."

Television's road was indeed uneven in those early years, but its growth as an advertising powerhouse was undeniable and inexorable, and this new power was evident in the increased coverage TV advertising and programming received in the pages of *Ad Age*.

The second half of the 1940s also saw *Ad Age* increasingly monitor the advertising volume of the agencies. It began its annual ranking of agencies by billings in January, 1945, when it published its first listing of the largest agencies. There were only 22 shops profiled in that first compendium, with combined U.S. billings of about $475 million for 1944. J. Walter Thompson led the pack with $72 million. Young & Rubicam was a distant second at $51 million, with N. W. Ayer & Son, McCann-Erickson and Foote, Cone & Belding rounding out the top five. By comparison, in *Ad Age's* 1991 income and billings report, its 47th, the 500-plus agencies reporting had U.S. billings in 1990 of $54 billion, more than a thousand times the '45 figure!

By the end of the 1940s, all three Crain publications were prospering, although *Ad Age*, with a circulation of 21,000 and growing national respect, was clearly the company flagship. *Hospital Management* had become the paid circulation leader in the hospital field, however, and *Industrial Marketing* had put its Depression era woes behind it.

The company had outgrown its quarters at 100 E. Ohio St. and in mid-1950 moved three blocks to 200 E. Illinois St. Its new home was one floor of a converted brick warehouse a block east of Michigan Avenue and still close to the Chicago offices of most of the major advertising agencies.

"They remodeled the space for us," recalled Merle Kingman, who at the time was managing editor of *Industrial Marketing* and who later would serve in several capacities at *Advertising Age*, including features editor. "The architect who did the remodeling didn't like squared-off corners. We had all kinds of wedge-shaped angles to the walls, which meant the desks and other furniture never seemed to fit right." Odd angles or no, 200 E. Illinois was the Crain address for more than a decade, until the company moved into the building it occupies today at 740 N. Rush St.

The family business was prominent in the lives of the Crain boys as they were growing up. Here, G.D. and Gertrude dine with sons Keith (left), 9, and Rance, 11, in Los Angeles in 1950 while attending a meeting of the National Association of Broadcasters.

Despite *Hospital Management's* relative success in the Postwar years, G.D. Crain continued in his desire to get rid of the magazine, and in 1952 he found a buyer—Clissold Publishing Co. In a column in the June, 1952, issue of *HM*, he announced the ownership change, saying that "My own publishing activities . . . have become so diversified in recent years that I feel unable to give *Hospital Management* the increased time and attention which its importance in the development of the field will require from now on."

In a conversation with his son, Rance, in 1970, he gave a more pragmatic reason for shedding the monthly, however: "I sold *Hospital Management* . . . although it was doing very well at the time, simply because it competed with too many of our potential and actual advertisers. I felt that it put us in an inconsistent position to be soliciting business from publishers with whom we were competing. And actually we got substantial business later from publications for *Ad Age* and *IM* that we never could have done business with as long as we were publishing *Hospital Management*."

So G.D. Crain once again was the owner of just two publications—if only for the moment.

Chapter 9

The Depression's 'Child' Grows Up

We're off on a new adventure!
—G.D. Crain, February 1953

With typical enthusiasm, the 68-year-old publisher heralded the arrival of his new monthly magazine, *Advertising Requirements,* which rolled off the presses as Dwight D. Eisenhower was beginning his eight-year tenancy in the White House as the first Republican President since the Great Depression. Crain said in the first issue that *AR* would be "devoted to all things an advertising or promotion manager does besides buying time or space in advertising media. Half of America's advertising dollars—and we suspect far more than half of American admen's time and talents—are devoted to art and production, to printing and paper and direct mail, to premiums and novelties and shows and exhibits, to sales meetings . . . or point of purchase promotions."

In the magazine's maiden effort, a 102-page issue that anticipated the growth of direct mail and sales promotion (its title would in 1961 be changed to *Advertising & Sales Promotion*), articles included "The ABC's of Couponing," "The Payoff Point in Point of Purchase" and "10 Ways to Stretch Your Art Budget." This editorial thrust affirmed the promise Crain made in that publisher's note that "We aim to give you here a down-to-earth book, filled with material you can apply directly to your work. We will steer clear of the theoretical and the discursive. Instead, we will bring you how-to-do-it information and important product and technique developments, in simple, easy-to-get-at style."

As the company has done so often, it relied heavily on the talents and expertise of staff members in starting new publications and strengthening existing ones. Many times, this resulted in split duties. For instance, Sid Bernstein, editor of *Advertising Age*, also assumed the title of editorial director of the new *Advertising Requirements*, and Stan Cohen, Washington editor both of *Ad Age* and *Industrial Marketing*, filled the same position with *AR*.

Bernstein's *AR* appointment gave him yet another hat to wear. Only a year earlier, he had been named editorial director of *IM*, replacing Bob Aitchison, who left the magazine to become a partner in a Chicago advertising agency. The idea behind Bernstein's selection, according to the announcement in *IM*, was "to assure coordination of the editorial staffs [of *AA* and *IM*], and particularly to strengthen the news coverage of *Industrial Marketing* through utilization of the large field staff of *Advertising Age*. This arrangement will also assure increased coverage of industrial advertising and marketing activities in *Advertising Age*."

This synergy was not restricted to the editorial side of Crain publications; members of the sales staffs sometimes were expected to cross over as well, especially inasmuch as *Ad Age* in those years carried healthy amounts of trade magazine advertising—including many of the same publications that also advertised in *IM*. Longtime employee and Crain executive Arthur E. Mertz, who was in sales for *Ad Age* during those years, said that "The *Ad Age* guys were trying to sell *Industrial Marketing*, too. It was easier to sell *Ad Age*, though, so we didn't give *IM* as much of our time as we should have."

Indeed, *Ad Age* was the company flagship in every sense through the booming Eisenhower years, years that saw the explosion of television and a burgeoning suburbia spurred by the Baby Boom as dual cultural hallmarks of the era. *AA's* paid circulation had grown steadily since the end of the war, pushing through the 20,000 level in 1948 and the 30,000 plateau in December, 1954, the eve of its 25th anniversary. As it grew both in circulation and advertising—issues of 120–150 pages were not uncommon in the mid-1950s—arch-rival *Printers' Ink* rapidly slipped from its perch as king of the hill and in less than 20 years would be only a memory.

Advertising Publications Inc. was still a relatively small operation, consisting of a Chicago headquarters, where all three magazines were edited and where the then-small circulation and accounting departments were housed; a New York office in various Midtown locations

On the occasion of the 25th anniversary of *Advertising Age* and the 39th
anniversary of *Industrial Marketing*, G.D. Crain was honored by the
Chicago Industrial Advertisers Association (CIAA). Richard C. Christian,
president of the CIAA, presented him with a life membership in the
group as Keith Evans, director of marketing for Joseph T. Ryerson & Son,
looked on.

(successively, 801 Second Ave., 480 Lexington Ave., 630 Third Ave.,
708 Third Ave. before the 1981 move to its current quarters at 220 E.
42nd St.), consisting of about five *Ad Age* reporters and editors and a
sales staff of six and one *Industrial Marketing* editor plus an Eastern
sales manager; and a Washington bureau where Stan Cohen held
forth as the lone editorial presence. As befitting the company's size,
the operations—and the chain-of-command—often were informal.

Jarlath (Jack) Graham, *Ad Age* managing editor from 1953 to 1969
and later co-editor, recalled one episode in which G.D. Crain was dis-
turbed over the paper's failure to cover a breaking Chicago advertising story. "I told him we had four things going at the same time and
only three reporters," Graham said. "I thought this [the one that
wasn't staffed] was the least important, but it turned out to be the big
one and we missed it. His response: 'If you need another reporter, go
hire one.'

"So I went to [editor] Sid Bernstein with the news that G.D. had
okayed our adding to the staff. His answer: 'You're not going to hire
another reporter.' And we didn't."

Similarly, Art Mertz said that when he was on the *Ad Age* sales staff, Crain called him into his office one day and without any preamble awarded him Cleveland—a major center for *Ad Age* advertising—as an added territory, but neglected to inform Mertz's boss, Sales Manager Gorden Lewis, of the decision. "When I told Gorden I'd been given Cleveland, he was miffed and said 'Okay, I'm taking Milwaukee away from you.' The net result for me was a wash—no gain," Mertz said.

With sons Rance and Keith in high school during the '50s, Gertrude Crain began, at her husband's urging, to take a larger role in the company. "I was always interested in business, and he was anxious for me to learn more because we were a small family company," she said. "And so gradually, I started going down to the office. In the beginning, I used to sign the payroll, and then, by degrees, I got to know more and more about the business."

Gertrude Crain shares one of her husband's hobbies, fishing, at Lac La Croix in Canada, circa 1950.

S.R. Bernstein, whose Crain career has spanned nearly 70 years, is shown here (left) receiving the Chicago "Advertising Man of the Year" award in 1958 from Joe Guenther of Branham Co. Sid Bernstein's titles have included: managing editor, *Hospital Management*; managing editor, editor, editorial director, and publisher, *Advertising Age*; and executive vice president, president, and chairman of the executive committee of Crain Communications, the last of which he still holds.

And the Crain sons weren't far behind their mother: by the early 1960s, both were active in the company themselves, Rance on the editorial side as an *Ad Age* reporter, first in Washington and then in New York, and Keith on the sales side, first with *Advertising & Sales Promotion* and later with *Ad Age*.

In August, 1958, *Ad Age* further solidifed its increasingly strong position as an advertising-marketing publication by purchasing the biweekly *Advertising Agency* magazine (formerly *Advertising Fortnightly*) from Bristol, Conn.-based Moore Publishing Co., and folding it.

"They were on the ropes and ready to go out of business," G.D. Crain said years later. "We bought the magazine because it increased our circulation a little and gave us some interesting features." *Ad Age's* article about the sale said it would result in about 4,000 new subscriptions, "bringing *AA's* total net paid to more than 46,000—by far the largest circulation ever attained by an advertising and marketing publication."

That same summer saw another benchmark: The first-ever "*Advertising Age* Summer Workshop on Creativity in Advertising," which, as the *Advertising Age* Creative Workshop, continues to this day as an annual event. That original three-day meeting, the brainchild of Sid Bernstein and Northwestern University Professor Steuart Henderson Britt, drew more than 350 agency, advertiser and media people from across the country to Chicago's Edgewater Beach Hotel for the sessions on creativity in print, radio and TV. And this was no hail-fellow-well-met convention; the program began at 9:00 each morning and went until 10:00 or later at night.

Among the highlights were iconoclastic California adman Stan Freberg, who blasted what he called "dull" radio creativity; well-known researchers Alfred Politz, Ernest Dichter and Burleigh Gardner in a panel discussion; a "gloves-off" critique of current print advertising; and a trip to the WGN-TV studios for a session devoted to the technical aspects of producing and editing television commercials.

Bernstein, who earlier in the year had been made *Ad Age* editorial director, said the idea for the workshop arose in part because of his experiences at annual meetings of the 4As (American Association of Advertising Agencies). "Here were people who employed all the creative people in America, but they weren't giving them any creative stuff," he said. "The sessions were all management-type meetings. There were client considerations and government affairs and that sort of thing, but there was very little creative activity. Creative people had nobody to talk to about their own business, about making ads."

In the first years of the Creative Workshop, it was run by Bernstein and Britt, not by Advertising Publications Inc., although the company later took over the operation, which has stayed a summer event, held either in Chicago or New York. It quickly became international in nature. "I think it still is—and has been for 25 years or so—the only international discussion opportunity for creative people," Bernstein said in 1990. "One year, we had 104 people from London alone, who came over on a chartered plane."

The growth of the company in general and *Ad Age* in particular caused it to outgrow its cramped quarters at 200 E. Illinois St. and in April, 1962, to buy the seven story building at 740 Rush St., which remains its Chicago office to this day (although the company later sold it and today is only a tenant). Art Mertz had an unusual memory of the building in an earlier day: "It had been the Methodist Publishing Co., and I'd called on them as an *Ad Age* salesman. In those days, the elevators used to work with a rope. The elevator was a cage, and there was a hole in one wall. You reached out through the hole, tugged on the rope, and the car went up!" In the beginning, the Crain publications occupied only a single floor of their new building (which by this time had enclosed, non-manual elevators).

Keith Crain became building manager, and was faced with the challenge of renting out its other floors. "We promoted it as the 'advertising center of Chicago' to differentiate it from other Class B buildings," he recalled. "And we were successful. We got *Popular Mechanics*, Abelson & Frankel [a sales promotion agency], General Bindery, Einson Freeman, and some other agencies."

The year 1962 also saw major personnel shifts at *Ad Age*: John Crichton, who had been named editor in 1958 when Bernstein was elevated to editorial director, left to become president of the American Association of Advertising Agencies, and the post of editor would be vacant for seven years. Also, Fred Danzig, a TV reviewer and feature writer with United Press International, joined *AA* in New York as senior editor and would rise to become executive editor (1969) and editor (1984).

The early, pre-Vietnam War Sixties was a heady era in the advertising world, yet a sober time for the nation. It was a "golden age of creativity," with such giants as David Ogilvy, William Bernbach and Mary Wells Lawrence turning out lively, breakthrough campaigns for, among others, Hathaway shirts, Avis rental cars and Braniff Airways, respectively.

But all the prosperity of the period and all the exuberance of these and other "what-will-they-do-next?" campaigns was more than offset by the assassination in November, 1963, of President John F. Kennedy and the pall that it cast over the country.

Vice President Lyndon B. Johnson succeeded to the presidency, bringing with him a "Great Society" social program and an era of "consensus"—for the moment—that helped him steamroll to victory over Republican Barry Goldwater in the 1964 election.

The year 1964 also marked a changing of the guard of sorts at Advertising Publications Inc. In May, G.D. Crain assumed the title of chairman, a new post, and Sid Bernstein was named both president of the company and publisher of *Advertising Age*, the latter a position Crain had held since the founding of the weekly 34 years earlier.

PART IV

NEW PUBLICATIONS, NEW CHALLENGES

1965–1977

Chapter 10

Branching Out

The biggest single problem . . . is remaining alert
and aggressive and not being smug and complacent.
                                        —G.D. Crain Jr., 1970

Smugness and complacency were hardly traits that could be ascribed to G.D. Crain, who indeed remained both alert and aggressive as his company moved into the mid-1960s. Now an octogenarian, he not only continued going to the office daily, but he also constantly sought new ways to expand his modest but thriving publishing operation.

One new venture was the short-lived *Marketing Insights,* a weekly magazine targeted to college students of marketing, advertising, and journalism and their instructors. Appearing only during the school year, and with minimal advertising support, it began in the fall of 1966 and ceased publication in the spring of 1969.

But the failure of *Marketing Insights* was more than offset by the ultimate success of the next Crain start-up, *Business Insurance,* which debuted in October, 1967. "It was an idea G.D. had carried around for about 50 years," said Alfred Malecki, who was *Business Insurance's* first advertising director and its publisher from 1970 until the end of 1991. "In his early years in Louisville, he was a stringer for a lot of publications, one of which was *Western Underwriter,* which is now *National Underwriter.*"

Malecki said Crain felt that all insurance publications were aimed at the *sellers* of insurance—agents, brokers, underwriters, and claims people in the industry. But there was nothing serving the information and decision making needs of the *buyer* of business insurance—

Business Insurance, begun in 1967, was "an idea G.D. (Crain) carried around for about 50 years," said Alfred Malecki, who was its publisher from 1970 until the end of 1991. In recent years, *BI* has been one of Crain Communications' most successful publications.

corporate consumer, risk manager, benefits manager, or whatever title—who pays the premiums for the company's insurance.

Malecki remembers that he, Rance Crain, and Myron (Mike) Hartenfeld, the company's vice president and business manager (and *BI's* publishing director at the outset), were sent out by G.D. Crain to visit "major players" across the country in the business insurance field. "We didn't get a uniformly positive response," he said. "There were many doubters who said 'there's not enough news [to warrant such a publication].'"

But G.D. Crain pushed ahead with the project. The first issue of *BI* was dated October 30, 1967. The lead editorial, headlined "Why Business Insurance?", set forth the new tabloid's mission:

> "It will be our purpose to provide our readers with a fortnightly package of the latest news and developments affecting the buyer of business insurance. In the issues to come, our staff will report on interviews with corporate insurance managers across the country about the specifics of their insurance setup— the types of coverage they have, how they communicate employee benefits to their workers, whether they self-insure in the form of higher deductibles, and other facets . . . We've given ourselves a big assignment, we know. But with the help of insurance buyers, brokers and insurance company officials, who form the nucleus of our readership and whom we've asked to keep us posted on developments at their companies, we hope to provide a continuing parade of ideas which *Business Insurance* readers can adapt to their own operations."

Rance Crain was *BI's* first editor, serving in that position until June 1970, when he became corporate editor of all Crain Communications publications. He was succeeded as *BI* editor by Richard Bjorklund, who resigned in 1972 and was succeeded by Stephen Gilkenson. Initial circulation was about 31,000, all of it controlled (unpaid). Currently, circulation is over 50,000, of which 35,000 is paid. In the first full year of operation, 1968, the publication carried 440 pages of advertising, aided by an incentive program, according to Malecki.

"*BI* represented quite an investment for a small company," Malecki said. "At one point, G.D. almost killed it. He thought it would grow faster. It was in the red more than $400,000 before it saw black ink in 1970."

Malecki remembers one board meeting at which he felt the fortnightly's fate hung in the balance "until Sid Bernstein said simply, 'Of course, there's no question about our continuing *Business Insurance.*' " From then on, the company was fully committed to *BI*, which grew steadily both in ad linage and circulation and today is one of the strongest titles in the Crain stable.

While *BI* was struggling through its start-up period in late 1967, the company made its first purchase: Chicago-based American Trade Magazines (ATM), publisher of *American Drycleaner* and *The American Laundry Digest,* two pocket-sized monthlies for owners of dry cleaning establishments and laundries respectively. Two more magazines were soon added to the ATM stable: *American Coin-Op,* a monthly for owners and operators of washing, drying and related services; and *American Clean Car,* a bi-monthly for owners and operators of car washes, both of which were acquired from United Business Publishers in the early 1970s.

These four publications would form what eventually became known as the American Trade Magazines Division of Crain Associated Enterprises Inc., a subsidiary of the parent company. Under Publisher Edwin Goldstein, they continue today to be a vital and profitable arm of the company based at 500 N. Dearborn Street, Chicago.

The year 1968 was a wrenching one for America. Martin Luther King Jr. was shot dead in Memphis in April, and two months later, Senator Robert F. Kennedy of New York was assassinated in a Los Angeles hotel while campaigning for the Democratic nomination for President. Immediately after Kennedy's death in June, *Advertising Age* spearheaded an aggressive anti-gun campaign with a June 10 editorial titled "Guns Must Go." One week later, *Ad Age* ran a second anti-handgun editorial with the same headline, this time on Page One. And later editorials urged readers to write their congressmen urging the enactment of gun-control legislation.

"The morning after Kennedy's shooting, both Sid [Bernstein] and I came into the office outraged," said Jack Graham. The upshot was the series of editorials, including the one Graham believes was the first the weekly had ever run on Page One.

"Two guys from North Advertising in Chicago [later Grey-North] were equally outraged," Graham said. "They drew up six anti-handgun ads, and they also prepared tape and film versions for radio and TV. Don Nathanson, president of the agency, agreed to foot the bill and offer these ads in a kit for anyone who wanted to use them in their community, and *Ad Age* ran the ads on a spread, along with a coupon."

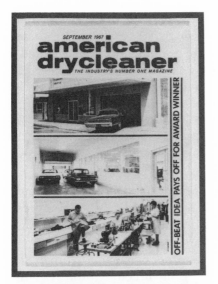

In 1967, Crain Communications made its first purchase: Chicago-based American Trade Magazines (ATM), publisher of *American Drycleaner* and *The American Laundry Digest,* pocket-sized monthlies for owners of dry cleaning establishments and laundries. In the early 1970s, ATM added *American Coin-Op,* a monthly for owners and operators of washing, drying, and related services, and *American Clean Car,* an every-other-monthly for owners and operators of car washes. The latter two titles were acquired from United Business Publishers.

Reader reaction was mixed, to say the least. Graham recalls that the coupon, which ran for several weeks, drew strong response. But there was plenty of negative response, too. "We accumulated two huge folders of hate mail, much of it with exactly the same wording," he said.

The most vitriolic among the letters *Ad Age* printed read, in part: "*AA's* vicious diatribe against guns was notable for its gross hysteria and complete absence of coherence. As a sportsman, I was at first angered...but as I read, the sad and grim reality became apparent—*AA* had gone berserk. The tragic vision of a slobbering loon lashing a typewriter was a sobering one..."

The advertising fallout was minimal, according to both Graham and Art Mertz of the *Ad Age* sales staff: The regular schedule of 1-inch ads for the National Rifle Association's *American Rifleman* magazine was canceled.

As 1968 drew to a close, so too did the career of a major figure in *Ad Age's* impressive Postwar growth—advertising director Gorden Lewis, who retired after 22 years with the company, all of them on the sales side and all of them in Chicago. Although G.D. Crain was fundamentally a writer and editor, he knew acutely the importance of having strong sales people, and Lewis was indeed strong.

"*Advertising Age* under him worked a hell of a lot harder at selling ads than its competition did," said Art Mertz, who reported to Lewis. "He developed a lot of promotions, direct mail, house ads. And he got things automated on the sales side. He contracted with two women who kept track of every ad in every competing book, something that's done with computers now. As a result, *Ad Age* sales people were far better armed than their competitors.

"He worked all the time," Mertz continued. "He went to a lot of conventions, and he never stopped selling. He'd have some guy cornered at 2 A.M. in the hospitality suite at a newspaper ad managers' convention telling him why his ad should be in *Ad Age*, not *Printers' Ink*."

Mertz also said Lewis went through the *Ad Age* rankings of the top 100 advertisers and top 100 agencies and found out who in each of them was a subscriber. He then had them—and their titles—assembled in a booklet that each member of the sales staff carried as evidence of *Ad Age's* reach and influence. "It was the best sales tool we had," Mertz said.

Mertz remembers his years in *Ad Age* sales, beginning in 1948, as a free-wheeling, hard-driving era in which advertising salesmen traveled more than they do today. "They [media companies] didn't want salesmen if they couldn't drink, because the customers drank, too," he said. "They wanted a guy who could drink but didn't show it."

He recalled his first encounter with Jack Gafford, a colorful and productive salesman in *Ad Age's* New York office and the publication's ad director in the '50s and '60s. "We were at a sales meeting in Louisville, and I ran into him in the hotel elevator one morning. He invited me to breakfast in the men's grill. It was about 7:30 or 8:00, and he ordered clams, a milkshake, and a beer. I'll never forget it.

"My territory was the Dakotas, Minnesota, and Wisconsin—a lot of small towns," Mertz continued. "We didn't generate much business in those places, maybe some small ads from newspapers or a radio station here and there, but *Ad Age* wanted us to make these calls to keep our profile high."

One of the few big cities in Mertz's territory during those years was Minneapolis. "I was competing with John McFadden, a salesman for *Printers' Ink,* trying to get an ad schedule from 3M for a new audio tape—they were only going to give the business to one of us. I got some of the new tape, and also got hold of the music from the 'Dragnet' TV show. Then I made my sales pitch on the tape by mimicking McFadden—he talked like Jack Webb on 'Dragnet'—and I interspersed it with the 'dum-dah-dum-dum' music. The people at 3M thought it was great, and *Ad Age* got the business."

With Richard Nixon newly installed in the White House and *Advertising Age* about to complete its fourth decade, the weekly announced major staff changes that underscored its bipolar nature: New York-based James O'Gara, who had been executive editor, and Chicagoan Jack Graham, the managing editor, were both named editors of the publication. Succeeding O'Gara as executive editor was Fred Danzig, located in New York, while Don Morris, based in Chicago, took over Graham's former post as managing editor.

Another change, subtle but important, was made as the 1960s drew to a close: The corporate name was changed in July, 1969, from Advertising Publications Inc. to Crain Communications Inc., reflecting the company's diversity—a diversity that would only increase in the years ahead.

Chapter 11

The Old Order Changeth

The seventies will be a time of new beginnings,
a time of exploration both on earth and in the
heavens, a time of discovery.
    Richard Nixon, State of the Union address, 1970

The 1970s were indeed a time of change in the U.S.—for both good and ill. On the heels of the historic moon landing in 1969, space exploration became a high priority on the national agenda despite a recession, and by 1972, a dozen astronauts had been on the moon's surface.

The 1970 census showed California to be the most populous state, and the national head count also registered another first: more Americans now lived in suburbs than in the central cities.

The growing concern about the environment led to the first Earth Day in April, 1970, with demonstrations across the country against pollution and misuse of natural resources. And a month later, another demonstration—this one protesting the Vietnam war—ended in the fatal shooting of four students on the campus of Kent State University by Ohio National Guardsmen. American involvement in the agonizing and controversial Vietnam conflict lessened as our military presence there was reduced throughout the early 1970s, although the U.S. casualties in the war had been staggering: about 55,000 killed and 300,000 wounded.

Against this wildly varied backdrop of Nixonian optimism and anguished concern over foreign military intervention and the environment, Crain Communications entered the new decade. *Ad Age*, now with a circulation of 65,000, announced a big birthday without fanfare on January 12: An unobtrusive box at the bottom of Page One stated that "...*Advertising Age* marks completion of its 40th year and the start of its fifth decade of reporting the news of the advertising-marketing business."

Although *Ad Age* was low-keyed in acknowledging a major milestone, it was steadily broadening its reach and influence nationally. Executive Editor Fred Danzig had seen the publication grow from a more narrowly focused trade journal in the early '60s to one that was read by congressmen, corporate executives, and the financial community.

"When I started [at *Ad Age*], we as reporters usually only called people in the business," Danzig said. "Outside of our perimeter of sources, we would have to explain who we were. But in about 1969 or 1970, we began to bring in the 'civilian' world, and this led to *Ad Age* becoming more widely known in the business community."

This change, he said, was caused in part because advertising agencies began to go public and diversify into non-advertising businesses, which attracted the interest of Wall Street. Also, the rise of the consumer movement, spearheaded by Ralph Nader and other activists, focused national attention both on ad agencies and advertisers, and increased the interest in such governmental regulatory bodies as the Federal Trade Commission.

Longtime *Ad Age* Washington Bureau Chief Stan Cohen also credited the consumer movement of the 1970s as a major factor in raising *Ad Age's* profile, particularly in the nation's capital. "Because of our coverage, we started getting read a lot more by lawyers, federal regulators, and Congressional staffs," he said.

Ad Age also broadened its coverage to include fashion, sports, and show business, including radio and TV talent, all of which had strong advertising and marketing implications, Danzig added.

Major shifts were made at executive levels within the company during 1970. They included:

- David J. Cleary, an 18-year *Advertising Age* employee and most recently a Crain Communications Inc. vice president and vp-sales on the weekly, became the third publisher in *Ad Age* history, succeeding Sid Bernstein, who remained Crain Communications president.

- Rance Crain, who had been editorial director of *Advertising & Sales Promotion* and *Industrial Marketing,* as well as *Business Insurance* editor, was named editorial director of all CCI publications, including *Ad Age.*

- Keith Crain was named publisher of *Industrial Marketing.* Keith, who had moved to the *Ad Age* sales side in 1965, had been named publisher of *Advertising & Sales Promotion* in 1968. ("I complained about the quality of the magazine to my Dad, and he said 'Okay, you be the publisher.' ")

A new challenge was presented to Keith Crain just a year later. *Automotive News,* a weekly trade paper for the auto industry that had been run by the Slocum Publishing Co. of Detroit since 1925, was on the block.

"Sid Bernstein had corresponded with the Slocums for many years," Keith recalled. "In the fall of '70, we, among others, got a packet [of information about *Automotive News*]. Mrs. Slocum, who was a widow, was very ill, and they wanted to sell. The bidding came down to us and Fairchild Publications, and we decided to up the ante another $50,000. That convinced them to sell to us. I said, 'I'll run it—even though I've never been in Detroit in my life.' " Thus began Crain operations in Detroit, where today the company is a major presence.

The purchase of the 46-year-old *Automotive News* took effect with the June 7, 1971 issue, with Keith Crain as publisher. At the beginning, it was operated through Marketing Services Inc., a Crain subsidiary that had been created when the 740 N. Rush St. property in Chicago was purchased.

"*Automotive News* had been losing about a half-million dollars a year; I moved here [Detroit] and set about putting it right," said Keith, whose previous primary interest in cars had been racing them. "I quickly found out the manufacturing end of the industry was even more interesting than racing. I became the functioning editor, ad director, and sales manager. I cut costs and increased revenues, and within six months, we were breaking even. And we've made money ever since."

In 1971, following a spirited bidding competition with Fairchild Publications, Crain Communications purchased the 26-year-old *Automotive News* from the Slocum family (a 1925 issue of the publication, then a daily, is pictured above). With Keith Crain as its Detroit-based publisher, the weekly tabloid, which had been losing about a half-million dollars a year, was breaking even within six months and has been one of the company's big profit-makers ever since.

The publication became more aggressive in both ad sales and news coverage. It opened overseas offices in Japan and Germany, and also set up an office in Nashville because of the growing concentration of auto manufacturing plants in the mid-South. Current paid circulation of *AN* is about 79,000.

The next addition to the company's publishing stable was home-grown. Al Malecki remembers that *Pensions & Investments* was spawned at a lunch he had with Sid Bernstein and Rance Crain in early 1973. "They were trying to decide between introducing a publication on real estate and one on pensions, and Rance decided to go with pensions," he said. " 'We want you to start it,' they told me. 'How long will it take you to put a detailed proposal together?'

"Recklessly, I answered that I could do it in two weeks," Malecki continued. "Somehow I got it done and presented it to the board in April, and they approved it. Steve Gilkenson, who already was editor of *Business Insurance*, became editor of *P&I* as well. We had a pilot issue in July, and a first issue October 29."

"The idea for *P&I* really derived out of *Business Insurance*," Rance Crain said. "At *BI*, we reported on the benefit side, but we really didn't have the opportunity to focus on the investment side of pensions and profit-sharing and tax-exempt funds. My dad was not particularly in favor of the start-up, but he said 'If Rance wants to give it a try, let's go ahead.' And we did.

"At first we had a real problem," Rance continued. "We couldn't get advertising. We simply didn't get enough ads until the fourth or fifth year. Two years in a row, we raised the ad rates 20% each and finally made it into the black."

The premiere issue of the every-other-weekly tabloid, dated October 29, 1973, was 52 pages, with advertisers including the Bank of New York, Bankers Trust Co., First National Bank of Chicago, Equitable Life Assurance Society, and a variety of other banks, brokerage houses, insurance companies and capital managers.

An editorial titled "Why *Pensions & Investments* is here" stated in part: "*Pensions & Investments* . . . this week begins going out to 26,000 executives responsible for the management of $283 billion in retirement fund assets, as well as billions more in other tax-exempt fund accounts . . . We feel there is a tremendous need for a news vehicle directed principally at executives responsible for this huge pool of capital.

"The fund manager is a most important individual these days. The

Pensions & Investments was started in 1973 (premiere issue above, a 1990 version at right) to focus on the investment side of pensions and profit-sharing and tax-exempt funds. The tabloid struggled initially; "We didn't get ads until the fourth or fifth year," Rance Crain said. "Two years in a row we raised the ad rates 20% and finally made it into the black."

investment performance of the assets he oversees—in the case of corporate funds, at least—has a direct bearing on his company's profits. In some cases, even, the asset value of his fund comes close to, matches, or exceeds the company's total worth."

The lead story in that first issue focused on the conflict among municipal pension funds, politicians and investment men over whether to invest in Israel Bonds, which were being vigorously pushed as part of a massive drive to support the Israeli war effort. Opponents said the bonds were a poor investment because of low yields compared with other available bonds.

Malecki remained publisher of *P&I* through its startup period and until 1976, when he returned to devoting his full attention to *Business Insurance*. Steve Gilkenson succeeded him as *P&I* publisher, and Michael Clowes, who had been manager editor, became editor.

G.D. Crain, now in his late eighties, spent less and less time in the office in his last years, although the company's editors continued to get the familiar brief notes, fired off from his home in the Chicago suburb of Evanston, suggesting stories or leads to be tracked down. On November 7, 1973, he suffered a stroke and was taken to Evanston Hospital. He rallied, but never fully recovered, and died December 15 at the age of 88.

Major newspapers across the country, including *The New York Times* and the *Chicago Tribune,* carried obituaries on the founder of what had grown to be a business publishing empire and would become even larger in the years ahead. But the finest tribute to him, by longtime colleague Sid Bernstein, fittingly appeared in *Advertising Age*. In a signed editorial titled "G.D. Crain—the right kind of publisher," Bernstein wrote:

> "He had an enormous capacity for work and a relatively low tolerance for idling or chit chat, so he went at a furious clip all day long. Yet he seldom came in before ten in the morning or stayed much after five at night, and he snickered openly at those of us who took work home with us—something he never did...
>
> "He knew everyone in the business publishing field and the field of marketing to business and industry, an arena in which he ...[was] among the important founding fathers. But to me his most solid contribution to the business world was embodied in his firm belief in what I choose to call 'the editorial viewpoint'— the constant desire to be of genuine service to the reader of his publications, to provide honest mental nourishment for them, to

help them do a better job and thereby to provide a more useful, vital, important vehicle for advertisers...

"A great deal of the stature which the best business publications have achieved rests on the foundations built with such loving care, devotion, and attention to detail by men like G.D. Crain in his long lifetime of service to American business.

"We shall all miss him."

Chapter 12

Three Hits and a Miss

What Dad wanted for us was that the family stay
together and work together and build the company.
                                        —Rance Crain

In many family-owned publishing operations, the founder's passing from the scene has resulted in cataclysmic change or upheaval, often resulting in the company's sale or absorption by another entity. Such was not the case with Crain Communications Inc., where the leadership transition was smooth following G.D. Crain's death.

In fact, that transition had been evolving for years as G.D.'s active participation in the operations steadily lessened, while his wife, Gertrude, and sons Rance and Keith all had been increasing their own involvement.

Rance Crain had been elected Crain Communications president and editorial director in January 1973, with Sid Bernstein moving up to chairman of the executive committee. The move gave the elder Crain brother day-to-day operating responsibility, while Bernstein concentrated on expansion and acquisition activities. Then in January, 1974, Gertrude Crain, who had been corporate secretary-treasurer, became chairman of the board, while Keith was elected to the secretary-treasurer slot.

The first corporate casualty of the post-G.D. Crain era was *Promotion*, the successor to *Advertising & Sales Promotion*. The periodical, founded in 1953 as *Advertising Requirements*, changed from magazine to tabloid format in 1972 and increased its frequency from monthly to every-other-week in 1972. But a lack of advertising, combined with increased paper costs and postal rates, caused *Promotion* to cease publication in May, 1974.

The company euphemistically termed *Promotion's* demise a "merger" with *Advertising Age*, given that many of its features would appear in *Ad Age*. There was some justification for the so-called consolidation, though: A study had shown that 85% of *Promotion's* audience also read *Ad Age*.

In October, 1975, G.D. Crain posthumously received an honor that by all rights should have been accorded him during his lifetime: He was one of three people elected to the American Advertising Federation's Advertising Hall of Fame. The others were Fairfax Cone, founder-chairman of the Foote, Cone & Belding advertising agency, and Artemas Ward, an early advertising executive who died in 1925.

In 1976, Crain Communications returned in a big way to the acquisition mode it had entered with the purchase of *Automotive News* in 1971: In less than two years, the company loosened its purse strings three times and doubled the number of its publications.

"It's always been our way to take advantage of opportunities as they came along," Rance Crain said, "and one came along in '76: McGraw-Hill had given up on its magazine *Modern Healthcare,* and they sold it to us for $200,000."

In the Bicentennial year, that figure may well have seemed exorbitant to some publishing observers for a monthly publication that had shown only moderate promise in its four years. (The magazine, targeted to administrators, financial executives and purchasing managers of hospitals and nursing homes, was born of a combination of two other McGraw-Hill publications, *Modern Hospital* and *Modern Nursing*.) *MH* proved a canny acquisition for Crain, however. The company immediately hired Charles Lauer, executive vice president of Family Media, to be *Modern Healthcare's* publisher and advertising director.

"What Rance saw in 1976 was a pressure building for healthcare insitutions to be more accountable," said Chuck Lauer, who continues as *MH* publisher today. "Healthcare executives were going to have to be better managers and learn about finance and purchasing."

This conviction of Rance Crain's was buttressed in the editorial in the August, 1976, issue of *MH*, the first under Crain Communications ownership: "...Our editorial platform is going to be that our reader—the healthcare executive—probably needs to be more broadly informed than any other member of the healthcare delivery team. He needs to know about all aspects of the business side of running his institution: building, financial, raising money, labor relations,

In 1976, McGraw-Hill sold the monthly *Modern Healthcare* to Crain for $200,000, which may have seemed exorbitant to some publishing observers. But with the subsequent growth of the healthcare industry, the magazine has proven to be a wise investment and is now a weekly.

training, public relations, purchasing. In general, the main purpose of *Modern Healthcare* is to continually point out new and more efficient ways of delivering healthcare services and how the high cost of medical care is hurting not only the system but the ultimate beneficiary of the system—the patient."

In a memo to all Crain employees dated June 16, 1976, Rance said, "We think that the healthcare field lends itself especially well to our kind of business news journalism. We have been reporting on the high cost of medical care in *Business Insurance,* and now we will be stepping up our coverage in this area."

"One of the things I particularly liked about the company was the total separation of the editorial and advertising operations," Lauer said. "Rance stressed that to me right from the start, and I've always believed firmly in that separation between 'church and state.' "

Modern Healthcare, with Rance Crain as editor-in-chief and Donald Johnson as editor, was far from an overnight success. Lauer recalled that "as we walked in the door [of *MH's* Chicago office], the entire ad sales staff resigned. They didn't like the idea of a new owner. So at the beginning, I *was* the ad staff. I zeroed in on key accounts and traveled all over the country. I even put on one sales pitch in a men's room once."

Like many Crain acquisitions and startups, *MH* was an initial drain on the company coffers. "The circulation was 75,000 when we bought the book," Lauer said, "but we dropped it to 40,000 because a lot of the people getting it didn't have fiscal responsibility within their organizations. We lost $360,000 over the first three years, but we made money the fourth year."

Another acquisition resulted from a chance meeting. "My life has been full of chance meetings," Rance Crain has said. "At an American Business Press (ABP) management conference on Long Island in 1975, I met Ernie Zielasko, the founder and editor of *Rubber & Plastics News* in Akron, Ohio."

"We had coffee and decided to exchange publications," Zielasko remembers. "A month or two later, Rance wrote me and asked if we'd be interested in selling [R&PN] to them. We said no."

Some background: In 1971, Zielasko, backed by a handful of other investors, formed Heer Publishing Co. and started *R&PN* to cover the rubber industry from the rubber capital, Akron, with Zielasko as editor and publisher, and Lowell (Chris) Chrisman, who joined six weeks after the first issue, as vice president-sales (advertising director).

It's official! Early in 1976, Ernie Zielasko (left) and Lowell (Chris) Chrisman (right) sold *Rubber & Plastics News* to Crain Communications. Keith Crain, who is shown signing his name to the agreement, said he wouldn't buy *R&PN* unless both men stayed aboard—which they did.

"We started as a fortnightly and became profitable by 1973," Chris Chrisman said. "We were up against two competing magazines, but in four years, we'd gotten an 80% market share of advertising."

Both Rance and Keith Crain were impressed by the success of *Rubber & Plastics News,* and they coveted the tabloid, to the extent that they went to Akron to make an offer.

Zielasko and Chrisman were flattered, but they resisted the offer because, as Ernie Zielasko said, "We were afraid of losing our editorial independence. I had heard horror stories about small trade books being forced to compromise their editorial integrity after being sold to large publishing houses."

The Brothers Crain were not easily dissuaded. Thirty days after their initial visit, "We got a phone call from Rance—the ante had gone up, but we said no again," Chrisman said. "Every thirty days after that for months, like clockwork, we received an increased offer.

"In January [1976], we got a call from Keith. He said, 'All right, *you* put a price tag on it.' We did some research and came up with a figure, and Ernie and I went up to Detroit to see Keith. We walked into his office, and he said 'How much?' We told him our price, and he took it. But he said he wouldn't buy unless we both stayed. We did. And it was a purchase that paid off well for the Crains."

Why did Chrisman and Zielasko agree to the sale? "I finally concluded that [the Crains] followed the same publishing philosophy we did," Zielasko said. "Produce the best editorial product possible and advertising, in time, will come your way. So when Keith and Rance promised autonomy, we began to see advantages in selling."

The first issue of *Rubber & Plastics News* under Crain ownership appeared April 8, 1976. It was the beginning of what was to be a major presence for Crain Communications in the Cleveland-Akron area.

Even with two new acquisitions in 1976, the Crain appetite was not satisfied. In 1977, the company bought *AutoWeek,* a tabloid for car enthusiasts with a circulation of about 25,000, and two monthly tabloids, *Aviation News* and *The American Collector.* The seller was Real Resources Group Inc., Reno, Nevada, and the package also included a printing plant in Reno and a circulation fulfillment operation in Lafayette, California, both of which were later sold. *Aviation News* also was sold, and *The American Collector* ceased publication in 1979. (Crain undertook another collectibles publication, *The Collector-Investor,* in 1980, but it stopped publishing two years later.)

For Keith Crain, the *AutoWeek* buy was a natural. "I always thought the [Fairchild Publications] concept of *Women's Wear Daily* [a news publication] and *W* [a feature magazine on women's fashions] made a lot on sense," he said. The purchase of the racing-oriented *AutoWeek* gave Crain Communications, already owner of *Automotive News*, a similar synergy in the auto field.

The acquisition of *AutoWeek* marked a milestone for the company: After 61 years this was its initial foray into consumer publishing. In the April 27, 1977, issue of *AutoWeek*, in announcing the change of ownership, Keith Crain said, "We're . . . pleased to become a part of the specialized consumer press. Until now, publications of Crain Communications have always been business-oriented."

As with *Modern Healthcare*, this addition to the stable proved a wise move. *AutoWeek*, which was moved from Reno to Detroit two years after the purchase, switched from a tabloid to a slick magazine format in January, 1986, and has increased its sales tenfold to more than 265,000, making it Crains's largest circulation publication by far.

The company had made the plunge into consumer publications, and the water was just fine, thank you.

PART V

BROADENING THE HORIZONS

1978–1991

Chapter 13

The Crain Name Goes 'Public'

*We will make every effort to report the news of the
Chicago business scene as completely, promptly and
accurately as we know how.*
   —Crain's Chicago Business editorial, June 5, 1978

It all began with one of Rance Crain's "chance meetings":

"In 1977, I went to Houston to give a speech at the Houston Advertising Club," he said. "I spent an afternoon listening to Bob Gray, publisher of the *Houston Business Journal,* telling me how he developed *HBJ.* I figured if a business publication worked well in Houston, it would be twice as successful in Chicago."

The seed was planted. Rance Crain took the idea of a local business paper home to Chicago with him. He enlisted longtime *Advertising Age* sales manager Art Mertz to survey potential readers, advertisers, and advertising agency executives. "About 80% liked the idea," said Mertz, who would become the paper's first publisher.

Steve Yahn, who had been a financial writer with the *Chicago Daily News* and a senior editor at *Advertising Age,* was enlisted to help Rance develop a prototype, do the initial hiring, and get the paper going. "We wanted to call it *Chicago Business,*" said Yahn. "But another guy came out with a paper with a similar name [which was short-lived]. I told Rance he ought to put the Crain name on our publication to differentiate them, and he did."

At this point, Dame Fortune waltzed onto the dance floor. It was early 1978, and the *Chicago Daily News,* a hallowed name in American journalism for a century, was in its death rattle, yet another casualty of the trend away from metropolitan evening dailies. This left

Chicago with two major papers, the *Tribune* and the *Sun-Times,* both morning operations.

"At first, we were going to be an every-other-weekly," Rance said, "but when the *Daily News* went down, I called my brother Keith in Detroit and said I thought we should become a weekly. His answer was 'Let's go for it.' "

So *Crain's Chicago Business* was born, with Steve Yahn as editor. If the demise of the *Daily News* in the spring of 1978 was a marketing stimulus to *CCB* (as the new publication would be called), the fallen paper's former staff also provided a rich pool of talent.

"We rushed in and grabbed Dan Miller to be our managing editor," Yahn said, "with the understanding that he would eventually become editor. He had been automotive editor of the *Daily News,* and then assistant business editor. And we also got Sandy Pesmen, a *News* feature writer, whom we made our feature editor."

Yahn and his new staff, plus a large pool of freelancers, put together two lively prototypes—a "pilot" and a "co-pilot" issue—during the spring of 1978. Also that spring, Joe Cappo, a former *Daily News* marketing and general business columnist who had moved briefly to the *Sun-Times,* was hired to be *CCB's* editor-at-large, a role in which he wrote a weekly column and occasional other articles.

The first newsstand issue of the tabloid *Crain's Chicago Business* appeared on Monday, June 5, 1978 (cover price, 50 cents, $25 a year), a 46-page edition with a lead story—an exclusive—on how the Marshall Field & Co. department store chain was planning further suburban expansion. Among the charter advertisers in that first issue were *Time* and *Newsweek* magazines, Illinois Bell, National Car Rental and the Continental Plaza Hotel.

As part of the promotional fanfare for the new paper, Rance Crain stood amid the noise and bustle of Union Station handing out free issues to commuters during the morning rush hour. "While I was passing out copies, a newsstand vendor in the station came up to me," Rance recalled. "He said, 'I sure hope you don't have much of your own money tied up in this, because it's not going to work.' "

The vendor was not alone in his cynicism. The Chicago business community greeted the new journal with indifference or puzzlement at best, scorn at worst. "We would be working on stories and call sources, saying we were with *Crain's Chicago Business,*" Sandy Pesmen remembers. "They would say 'Who? What? The people who make the toilets?' Some thought we were the plumbing manufacturer [Crane Co.]. Pretty soon, we were introducing ourselves by saying,

VOL. 1, NO. 1   JUNE 5, 1978

Crain's Chicago Business

THE WEEKLY NEWSPAPER FOR MID-AMERICA

50c a copy; $25 a year • © Entire contents copyright 1978 by Crain Communications Inc. All rights reserved.

Marshall Field headed into Northbrook, Dundee

Building boom seen as part of plan to create national retailing network

By MARALYN EDID

Marshall Field & Co. will open stores in Northbrook Court and in a shopping center to be constructed in Dundee, CRAIN'S CHICAGO BUSINESS learned.

The store openings, scheduled for 1980, are part of Field's previously announced five-year plan to add four units in the Chicago area.

They also give credence to the retailer's claim—made last winter as Field's struggled against an unwanted tender offer from Carter Hawley Hale Stores—that Field's is growing into a national retailing power.

Field's will become the fourth anchor in the 130-store Northbrook Court shopping center, joining Sears, Roebuck & Co., Lord & Taylor and Neiman-Marcus, thus ending speculation as to whether and when the Chicago retailer would set up shop in the giant mall. The Northbrook store will cover approximately 150,000 square feet and offer merchandise like the Water Tower Place outlet, which emphasizes top-quality items and specialty shops.

Details on the Dundee project and the two other unnamed sites were not available.

Even in the face of disappointing earnings, Field's is aggressively pursuing its goal of becoming what president Angelo Arena describes as a "truly national company." For the year ended Jan. 31, the retailer reported profits of $15.9 million, or $1.76 a share, down 13% from a year earlier. First quarter earnings also fell this year to 1 cent a share from 2 cents. (Mr. Arena noted 1978 results reflected 2 cents a share in litigation costs associated with shareholder suits after the thwarted takeover attempt by Carter Hawley Hale Stores.)

Field's has announced plans to build five stores in the Houston area and agreed in principle to merge California-based John Breuner Co., a home furnishings and furniture rental company, into

Continued on Page 45

Chicago center of controversy

Fed meat-pricers move here

By PAUL MERRION

WASHINGTON—The U.S. government is sending the Navy to Chicago next month to secure better control over the government's meat purchases.

The move highlights a growing controversy about alleged price manipulation in the $38-billion-a-year meat industry. Most of the new and allegations are aimed at the industry's primary pricing tool—the Chicago-based Yellow Sheet, a twice-a-week price-reporting service that for most of its 87 years has been the bible of the industry.

The Yellow Sheet, which sells for $170 a year, is used by meat packers, grocery stores and other large buyers to determine wholesale prices on up to 90% of all meat sold in the U.S. An error in the Yellow Sheet price—caused either by manipulation or carelessness in reporting—could cost consumers millions of dollars.

Soaring beef prices led consumer prices sharply higher in May, both in Chicago and the nation.

And the world's largest institutional meat buyer—the U.S. government, at $800 million a year—

is moving its pricing operations to Chicago July 1 to be closer to the source of information, to avoid delays in price reporting and to generally keep an eye on things.

The Defense Subsistence Office, 55 E. Jackson, will assume responsibility for issuing weekly meat pricing guides for military commissaries around the world. The guides are used in ordering supplies and setting meat prices for military personnel.

The office currently has 15 employes, but it was not known whether new employes will be

Continued on Page 45

Searle R&D chief faces logjam

By SUSAN GUREVITZ

The expertise of G.D. Searle's newly appointed research chief will take Searle in a new direction, but his most pressing duty will be to jump out the right to 10 new drugs which already are in Searle's R & D pipeline, a source close to the company told CRAIN'S CHICAGO BUSINESS.

Because it usually takes between seven to 10 years to get a new drug through the FDA procedures and on the market, Dr. Daniel Azarnoff will "analyze what is

already available and emphasize those he can work with," the source noted.

Searle's new R & D chief: eager enough to forego a vacation. Page 44.

The drugs currently under consideration are most likely in the cardiovascular, renal and gastrointestinal areas. Dr. Azarnoff's areas of expertise include lipids and metabolism relating to hardening of the arteries, and pharmacokinetics—how the body

responds to drugs.

The source said that, ideally, Searle would like to produce two drugs a year.

It is anticipated that Dr. Azarnoff's only constraints will be budget, people and space. Searle spent $52.6 million on R & D last year and expects to increase that higher to $55 million this year. The R & D director does about 2% of the department's research and directs a research staff of more than 700 people.

Searle is "in better shape" than

Continued on Page 45

Highlights

Business columnist **Joe Cappo** makes his debut in CRAIN'S CHICAGO BUSINESS with a special plea to all outraged business people, uptight consumerists and indignant legislators: Quiet down. Joe bows in with his weekly column on:
Page 6

Kitsch on Boul Mich?

The quality of life on the Magnificent Mile appears to be slipping on fast-food restaurants, going-out-of-business signs and traffic jams. But merchants say the decline is more apparent than real. **Page 8.**

Local consumers steady

Chicago consumers aren't as eager as their national counterparts to cut back on their spending, market researcher Leo Shapiro & Associates reports. **Page 4.**

Joan Rivers' big gamble

Comedienne Joan Rivers has come a long way since her hectic Second City days. Today she's teetering on the precipice, with her home mortgaged and money borrowed to finance her first film, "Rabbit Test." For a report on Joan Rivers' career and the biggest gamble of her life, check "5-to-9". **Page 29.**

Lasser Beverages at 99

For 99 years, the Lasser family has operated its soda pop factory in the DePaul neighborhood and watched the area go through dozens of cycles. The neighborhood is in a revival mood now, and the present Lasser in charge sees an effervescent future. **Page 12.**

Late News

Schlitz bets on JWT

Chicago-based J. Walter Thompson advertising agency landed the $20 million Schlitz-brand beer account, formerly handled by Leo Burnett of Chicago. JWT was chosen from a field of six in competitive bidding conducted by Jos. Schlitz Brewing Co. of Milwaukee.

Northrop to hire 900

Northrop Corp., the largest defense contractor in Chicago, plans to hire 900 additional employes during the next year and a half at its Rolling Meadows facility. Earlier this year, Northrop received two large contracts from the Air Force to develop the electronic countermeasures systems for the F-15 fighter ($200 million) and the B-52 ($28 million).

Continued on Page 2

The first issue of *Crain's Chicago Business* (above) came out in 1978, soon after the demise of the *Chicago Daily News*. The death of the *Daily News* provided the new paper with a rich talent pool and also provided the stimulus for *CCB* to go weekly, rather than every other week, which was the original plan.

"Hello, this is so-and-so from *C-R-A-I-N's Chicago Business*." In those early days, she said, "I called in every chip that was owed me from 20 years in the newspaper business in Chicago."

The sales staff had its own sets of challenges. Gloria Scoby, an original *CCB* ad salesman and now the paper's publisher, remembered those early days with mixed feelings. "A lot of advertisers thought we were some kind of vertical trade book and expected stories [in exchange for advertising]. They didn't get those stories, though. And we also fought to be recognized as a newspaper, not a magazine."

CCB won the "we're-a-newspaper-not-a-magazine" battle, and won advertising in the process. But it wasn't easy. Scoby zeroed in on an office furniture dealer. "They ran a small ad in the *Wall Street Journal*, but nothing with us," she said. "I called them every day for three months, and they finally agreed to use us. Today, they're one of our top advertisers."

One of *CCB's* biggest assets was its physical appearance. "The first major sign of encouragement we got was for our lively, contemporary look," Steve Yahn said. "A lot of people said it looked as much like a book about a city as a financial publication. And that was exactly the intent—*CCB* was meant to be a 'hybrid' between a city publication and a financial publication."

This attractive hybrid was the design of Joe Faraci, the corporate art director. Faraci, who worked for the company for 30 years before his retirement in 1990, was responsible for the distinctive design of many of the Crain publications.

As attractive as *CCB* was, however, it was more than just a pretty face. From the start, it strove to build its reputation with enterprise reporting. "Rance loves scoops," Dan Miller said. "And the 'scoops mentality' became immediately ingrained in the culture of the new reporters we brought in."

One of those early scoops caused a firestorm that threatened to severely damage the new paper's reputation. In late July, *CCB* learned through sources in the Chicago advertising community that Sears, Roebuck & Co. planned to drastically curtail its advertising. The banner story on August 7, with the headline "Sears slashes TV, print ad budgets," stated that cuts could reach the $100 million mark. The giant retailer angrily denied the report. "They called it preposterous," Steve Yahn said. "As a result, we really suffered credibility problems around town. From early August until mid-October, we kept trying to find a way to get it back."

Then came the break that was to stunningly—and permanently—reverse the fledgling publication's fortunes. "A young Sears public relations man named Wiley Brooks came to see Rance on a job interview," Yahn said. "He wanted to be *CCB* managing editor [a slot that would open up according to plans when Dan Miller replaced Yahn as editor]. Brooks told Rance that our earlier article about Sear's ad cuts was true, that he had the proof, and that there was to be a massive reorganization of the company."

Brooks's proof was a voluminous, secret five-year plan referred to informally at Sears as the "Yellow Book." Brooks proceeded to leak the plan to *CCB* in three sections. "Each one cost *Crain's* a lunch at Nick's Fishmarket [a pricey Chicago eatery]," Yahn said. "I still remember sprinting through the downtown streets with the first part of the book in a manila folder. Our whole reputation for accuracy was on the line."

In a bylined piece by Yahn, *Crain's Chicago Business* broke the story of Sears's secret plan on December 4 with a highly detailed 10-page package that included charts, graphs, and numerous sidebars drawn from the plan. "It made our reputation," Yahn said. "TV picked up on it in a big way on the weekend before we hit the streets. And on Monday, copies were gone by 9 A.M. and newsstands were calling for replacements. We were interviewed by BBC and covered by *Business Week*, and *Business Week* was after us for original documents. Sears did not respond." (Brooks, who left the company and went to work for a newspaper, was not named as the source of the Yellow Book by *CCB*, but he was so identified by Donald R. Katz in his 1987 book about Sears, "The Big Store.")

CCB was off and rolling now, and it continued to go after exclusives aggressively. "Our idea was to scoop the dailies, to print news people hadn't seen before," Rance Crain said. "We pursued middle-sized companies because the dailies weren't covering them. We got great publicity for the Sears story; one national publication called us 'feisty.' In a way, that changed the perception of the company. Here in Chicago, we weren't well-known, but as we started getting scoops, we built our identity in the city."

In a vigorous promotional and advertising campaign on radio, TV, and transit boards, the paper stressed its "scoop orientation" and its overall aggressive approach to covering the news. "I took the business sections of the two Chicago dailies and measured the column inches of local business news and features," said Joe Cappo, who became

CCB publisher in May, 1979. "Then I measured *CCB*. Every week, we had more than the two papers combined." One result of Cappo's finding was a TV commercial that drove home the message that if you read *Crain's Chicago Business*, you didn't need the *Chicago Tribune* financial section.

That bare-knuckle commercial may well have spurred a top *Tribune* editor to lash out in a fit of pique during a news doping session at the *Trib*. One departmental editor mentioned a story that had run in *CCB*, and his superior angrily wheeled about: "Do me a favor, will you?" he snapped. "Next time you see a copy of *Crain's*, spit on it!"

The *Tribune* editor's reaction was one of many indications that *CCB* was indeed making inroads in the city, although its early days were far from easy. Both Joe Cappo and Dan Miller, who had become editor in November, 1978 (Greg David, formerly of *Business Insurance*, was the new managing editor), remembered the tough times. "There was a lot of suspicion of us at the beginning," Miller said. "When we called someone at a company, their attitude was, 'Why should we talk to them?' They thought we were their competition, trying to ferret out information."

"The category [city business] was not yet well developed when we started out," Cappo said. "In '78, there were something like only 15 regional and local business publications in the U.S. During our first year, the jury was still out; we racked up some big losses for that era. But after the first year, I had no doubt that we would make it. And by our third full year, 1981, we were profitable."

Dan Miller remembers when the publication turned the financial corner: "When we learned that we'd had our first profitable month, I went to Rance and congratulated him. He said, 'Great! Now we've got some money to put back into the editorial product.'"

Chapter 14

Milestones and Startups

*Our challenge, as we embark on our second 50
years, is to remain alert, aggressive and responsive
to the needs of our readers. We appreciate your
support . . . and pledge that we will always try to be
worthy of it . . .*
— Rance Crain, January 7, 1980

The above was the closing portion of Rance Crain's letter to readers in
the 50th anniversary issue of *Advertising Age*. The publication had
come a long way since its Depression-era beginnings, and at the beginning of the new decade, circulation stood at an all-time high of
77,000.

During the 1970s, *Ad Age* had enjoyed a circulation increase of
some 12,000 and experienced myriad changes. Among them:

- In 1977, it got a new publisher, Louis DeMarco, who had been advertising director. He succeeded David J. Cleary, who moved up to
group publisher, with responsibility for *Ad Age, Business Insurance,
Pensions & Investments* and *Modern Healthcare*.

- Also in 1977, James Brady became a weekly columnist after his
work attracted Rance Crain's attention. Brady, who had been publisher of *Women's Wear Daily*, editor and publisher of *Harper's Bazaar*, and editor of *New York* magazine, was a columnist and
associate publisher of Rupert Murdoch's *New York Post* at the time
he began writing for *Ad Age*. Fred Danzig recalled that both Rance
Crain and *Ad Age* Publisher Lou DeMarco saw in Brady, who was
so closely identified with New York, an opportunity to help combat
the perception in Manhattan that *Ad Age* was a "Chicago book."

"I didn't know if Murdoch would let me do it [write for *Ad Age*]," Brady said, "but I got a favorable reaction. He told me, 'That's fine, as long as you don't trash us.' " In November, Brady, who now also does a column for *Parade* magazine, began writing free-wheeling and wide-ranging essay columns for *Advertising Age* that quickly became one of the best-read elements in the publication. His column continues today, and as editor at large, also writes a "three-dot" people column, "Brady's Bunch," for *Ad Age*, plus a weekly column for *Crain's New York Business*.

- In May, 1977, international coverage was expanded with the debut of *Advertising Age Europe*, a monthly section. In January 1979, it became a freestanding publication, selling for $1.50 a copy. Advertisers did not flock to *AAE*, however, and it ceased publication in December of '79 after 12 issues as a stand-alone.

- Throughout the 1970s, broadcast news became an increasingly important segment in the *Advertising Age* editorial mix, in large measure because of the reporting of Maurine Christopher. Christopher, whose contacts and confidants included CBS founder William Paley and Ted Turner of Turner Broadcasting, was an *Ad Age* reporter and editor in New York for 44 years until her retirement in 1991.

- In 1978, "Section 2" was launched as a new feature element of *Ad Age*. These advertising-supported packages focused on single marketing and media topics each week, such as grocery marketing, healthcare, direct marketing, research, newspapers, and magazines. (In early 1982, Section 2 was merged into a pullout "Magazine" section that combined various feature elements of the publication. Later that year, the Section 2 name disappeared entirely, although the single-subject concept continued under the name "Special Report.")

Advertising Age was not making the only news in the company as the '80s began, however. In 1980, there were two start-ups, publications that were to have vastly different histories.

Buoyed by reader acceptance and to a lesser degree advertiser affirmation of *Crain's Chicago Business*, the company brought forth an offspring. "Ernie Zielasko and Chris Chrisman convinced us of the potential of a *Crain's Cleveland Business*," Keith Crain said. Chrisman undertook a feasibility study, which, as he said, "turned out to be positive." On March 31, 1980, the paper debuted as a fortnightly tabloid,

Encouraged by the success of *Crain's Chicago Business*, the company followed with three more business tabloids, *Crain's Cleveland Business* (1980), *and Crain's Detroit Business and Crain's New York Business,* which started within weeks of each other early in 1985.

which Keith said at the time demonstrated faith in the Greater Cleveland area, "a publication to rally around."

Crain's Cleveland Business had Keith as its president, Ernie Zielasko as publisher, and Chris Chrisman as director of sales, and it bore a strong physical resemblance to its older Chicago cousin early on. And, like the Chicago version, it was aggressive in its reporting of the local business scene.

A dramatic example of its enterprise reporting came on March 2, 1981, when the young paper, by now a weekly with a controlled circulation of 25,000, obtained a confidential list of 65 Cleveland-area suppliers to the ailing Chrysler Corp., along with their 1978 sales to the company, which totaled more than $550 million. At the time, there was speculation that Chrysler would go under and the *Crain's Cleveland Business* report was stark testimony to the economic impact on Northern Ohio that the giant automaker's demise would have had.

Chris Chrisman had been named publisher of *Cleveland Business* by mid-1980, while Ernie Zielasko moved up to publishing director and remained editor and publisher of Akron-based *Rubber and Plastics News*, allowing him to concentrate on "his first love," the Akron operation. And Chrisman, although moving his office to Cleveland, retained his post as director of sales at *RPN*.

"When we started *Crain's Cleveland Business*, the *Northern Ohio Business Journal* was our competition," Chrisman said. "Eighteen months after we started, we were splitting the advertising business with them, 50–50. Then we went weekly, and our sales took off. Three years after we began, they *[NOBJ]* moved to Columbus as a monthly called *Ohio Business*. We broke even after the first three years," Chrisman continued, "and now we're in the black."

The company was less successful with a magazine called *The Collector-Investor,* the premiere issue of which came out in May, 1980. Steve Yahn, the first editor of *Crain's Chicago Business*, was publisher of this handsome monthly, targeted to investment aspects at "the top end of the collectibles market," including art works, Oriental rugs, antique furniture, and rare coins.

"Part of the impetus [for starting *The Collector-Investor*] was that in the early '80s, a hot publishing category was magazines catering to the wealthy—*Architectural Digest, The New Yorker, Town & Country,*" Yahn said. Unfortunately for Crain Communications, recessions in 1980 and 1982 drastically reduced the amount of discretionary income in the higher brackets, and the new magazine's advertising shrunk accordingly.

C-I's Summer, 1982 issue (which would be its last), ran a box announcing Crain Communications' plan to sell the magazine and quoted Rance Crain as saying that "We've decided to concentrate our resources on several new publishing ventures." Those ventures included the *Electronic Media Edition* of *Advertising Age* and *Crain's Illinois Business.* (Although Crain Communications was unable to sell the magazine itself, it did sell the subscription list to New York-based *Art & Auction* magazine.)

In the meantime, the company's Chicago office had become enmeshed in a struggle over whether its editorial employees should be represented by a union. In November, 1980, the Chicago Newspaper Guild Local 71, an AFL-CIO affiliate, which also represented the *Chicago Sun-Times* and other publications, informed Crain Communications that it would be conducting an organizing drive among the company's editorial staffers.

The company, whose editorial departments had never been unionized, fought back vigorously. Todd Fandell, newly hired as assistant corporate editor and previously assistant financial editor of the *Chicago Tribune,* was placed in charge of the Crain efforts to repel the union challenge.

For three months, emotions ran high as a crossfire went on, with reporters and editors deluged in a blizzard of paper—informational memos, arguments, charges, and counter-charges coming from both sides. The secret balloting, held in Crain's Rush Street offices on February 18, 1981, resulted in a defeat for the union by a 32–20 count, with 15 of the voters challenged, 13 by the union and two by management. The outcome of the balloting—defeat for the union—ultimately was upheld by the National Labor Relations Board.

The year 1981 was an eventful one for Crain's Akron operation. In April, *Rubber & Plastics News* marked its 10th anniversary, and in October, the 99-year-old, London-based *European Rubber Journal,* a monthly covering rubber and related industries in the U.K. and on the Continent, was acquired by Crain Communications, in large measure through the efforts of Ernie Zielasko.

In *Rubber & Plastics News's* anniversary issue, benchmarks of the publication's first decade were highlighted. They included *RPN's* 1978 battle over First Amendment rights in a Federal court (see box), and the 1979 decision to go weekly by publishing *Rubber & Plastics News II,* an eight-page, newspaper tabloid without advertising that runs every-other-week, alternating with the fortnightly *RPN.* In an open letter to readers in the anniversary issue, Editor Zielasko reiterated standards held both by *RPN* and Crain Communications: "We have always believed that news stories must be reported objectively. The 'new journalism' in which the writer's biases and prejudices slant a story is not for us. Our personal opinions are confined to the editorial page where you, recognizing them as such, can make your own judgments as to their value."

Keith Crain's growing role was underscored in May, 1981, when he was named vice-chairman of Crain Communications, a role in which he shares responsibility for day-to-day operations of all the company's activities with his brother, Rance. Succeeding Keith as secretary-treasurer were Merrilee Crain, Rance's wife, as secretary, and Mary Kay Crain, Keith's wife, as treasurer.

In 1982, the company, which the year before had passed the $50 million mark in sales, initiated three new publications, all of them "line extensions" of existing titles:

- *Crain's Illinois Business,* a quarterly magazine that as its title indicated covered business across the state, began publication with the Winter 1982 issue. "It started as a 'flanker product' to *Crain's Chicago Business,*" said Joe Cappo, *CCB* publisher and also publisher of the new book. "But it didn't get the advertising support we hoped for." *CIB* ceased publication in early 1986 after 15 issues.

- *Advertising Age's Focus,* a monthly English-language magazine, edited from London, which was targeted to a "pan-European" audience of advertising creatives in the U.K. and on the Continent. It, too, failed because of a lack of advertising support. "It was ahead of its time," said its last editor, John Wolfe, now *Ad Age's* New York Bureau chief, referring to the economic unification of Western Europe in 1992. (In 1987, however, a weekly newsletter, *Advertising Age's Euromarketing,* was launched and circulates some 1,500 copies to advertising and marketing personnel, primarily in Britain and on the Continent.)

- *Electronic Media Edition* of *Advertising Age,* which debuted with a prototype issue March 8, 1982, and a premiere issue May 3, concentrated, as its first editorial stated, on news from "commercial TV, cable networks and systems, radio, programming, syndication, videotex, home video recorders and more." At first a physical near-clone of *Ad Age,* the tabloid weekly gradually developed a design character of its own as it distanced itself from its parent.

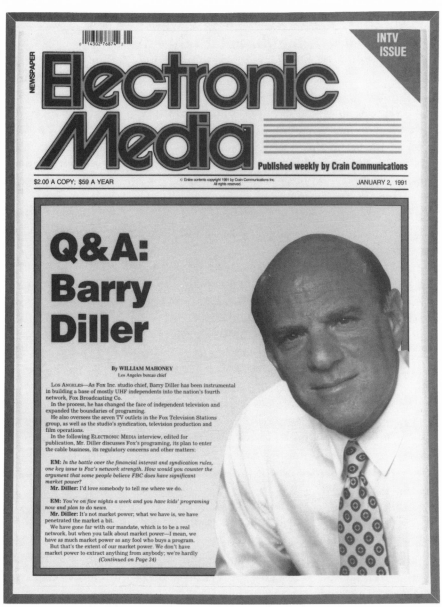

Q&A: Barry Diller

By WILLIAM MAHONEY
Los Angeles bureau chief

LOS ANGELES—As Fox Inc. studio chief, Barry Diller has been instrumental in building a base of mostly UHF independents into the nation's fourth network, Fox Broadcasting Co.

In the process, he has changed the face of independent television and expanded the boundaries of programing.

He also oversees the seven TV outlets in the Fox Television Stations group, as well as the studio's syndication, television production and film operations.

In the following ELECTRONIC MEDIA interview, edited for publication, Mr. Diller discusses Fox's programing, its plan to enter the cable business, its regulatory concerns and other matters:

EM: *In the battle over the financial interest and syndication rules, one key issue is Fox's network strength. How would you counter the argument that some people believe FBC does have significant market power?*

Mr. Diller: I'd love somebody to tell me where we do.

EM: *You're on five nights a week and you have kids' programing now and plan to do news.*

Mr. Diller: It's not market power; what we have is, we have penetrated the market a bit.

We have gone far with our mandate, which is to be a real network, but when you talk about market power—I mean, we have as much market power as any fool who buys a program.

But that's the extent of our market power. We don't have market power to extract anything from anybody; we're hardly

(Continued on Page 34)

Electronic Media, a weekly tabloid that began early in 1982 as an extension of *Advertising Age,* became independent of its parent later that year as it went about its role of covering "commercial TV, cable networks and systems, radio, programming, syndication, videotex, home video recorders, and more."

A Trade Publication Defends Its
First Amendment Rights in Court

Rubber & Plastics News Managing Editor Jacques Neher and his staff in Akron were closing an issue in March, 1978, when *RPN's* Washington Bureau reported it had obtained results of a National Highway Traffic Safety Administration (NHTSA) survey of 87,000 radial tire owners about tire defects. Firestone, with complaints running at nearly 4%, topped the list of the largest makers, according to the statistics.

This was big news, and *RPN* ran with the story, although a federal judge, at Firestone's request, had indefinitely extended a previously issued restraining order barring the government from releasing the results.

"I couldn't see any conflict," said Neher, who later would become editor of *Crain's Cleveland Business.* "The injunction was against the government, [not] a newspaper."

The day the story appeared in *RPN*, an attorney for Firestone subpoenaed Neher in an attempt to find out who leaked the story. Neher and Keith Crain, then Crain Automotive Group president, met with defense attorneys who said the outraged federal judge might throw Neher in jail. Crain said the attorneys warned him not to go into the courtroom because if the judge learned his identity, he, too, might be subpoenaed.

"My feeling was, 'The hell with that; if Jacques goes to court, I'll be with him,' " Crain said.

On the witness stand, Neher was asked, "Can you say whether or not the Department of Transportation was the source for this story?" Neher knew his position would be weakened if he pleaded the First Amendment to the wrong question.

"Yes, I can say *whether or not* the Department of Transportation was the source for the story."

The next question: "*Was* DOT the source?"

"I'm sorry, but I can't answer that question," the editor responded.

Neher had handled himself well. The judge, possibly seeking to avoid a delicate First Amendment confrontation, cited an obscure precedent stating that a reporter cannot be forced to reveal his sources until all other possible avenues are exhausted.

This meant, in effect, that Firestone would have to interrogate numerous NHTSA employees before the court could force Neher to answer the question. He had won his battle.

"I think in the long run, it was beneficial for the newspaper to go through something like that, both internally and to establish a reputation that the paper is not afraid to tell it like it is," Neher said later. "You'll tick some people off, but by and large you earn their respect."

In August, 1982, the words *Advertising Age* had disappeared from the title of what was now simply *Electronic Media;* the publication, which in its early days had shared both writing and editing staff members with *Ad Age*, began to build its own team.

Ron Alridge, who left his job as TV critic of the *Chicago Tribune* in May, 1983, to become *EM's* news editor, rose to managing editor a few months later and editor in June, 1984. He added the title of publisher in June, 1987, when David Persson left that post to become publisher of *Advertising Age*, replacing Lou DeMarco, who retired. (In 1991, Alridge's title became publisher-editorial director, with David Klein moving up to editor.)

Ron Alridge attributes *EM's* rapid growth to two major factors:

(1) Its publication in May, 1983, of a several-thousand-word excerpt from the Benjamin Report on CBS News's 90-minute documentary titled "The Uncounted Enemy: Vietnam." The documentary accused Gen. William Westmoreland and other military officials of deliberately underestimating enemy troop strengths in Vietnam before the Tet offensive, and Westmoreland's lawyers, as part of a $120 million libel suit against CBS, obtained by court order a copy of the report, which had been commissioned by the network. "Our publishing of portions of the report sent a powerful signal that we were going to be different from traditional trade publications," Alridge said.

(2) A strong focus on the program side of the business. "We started paying a lot of attention to programming and syndication, and almost instantly, we started feeling the impact," Aldridge added. That impact was particularly apparent in the advertising in issues coinciding with the National Association of Television Programming Executives (NAPTE) annual meetings. For instance, on February 9, 1984, *EM* published a 114-page issue, of which 57 were full page ads, most of them for programming. And in 1985, the January 3 and January 10 issues bulged with advertising and were a whopping 130 pages and 182 pages respectively.

By its third year, the weekly was in the black, and any doubts as to its ability to survive were dispelled. *Electronic Media* had arrived.

Chapter 15

Detroit Dynamics

The introduction of Crain's Detroit Business brings to four the number of Crain publications in Detroit, and gives our company 25 publications.
—Keith Crain, February 4, 1985

The 1980s was the decade of Crain Communications' greatest growth. The number of employees doubled, from 515 to 1,037, and net operating revenues soared, reaching more than $145 million by the end of the decade. Nowhere was the company's overall growth more in evidence than in the burgeoning Detroit operations, under the leadership of Keith Crain.

"Keith has always been oriented toward management, accounting, printing, and computers," Gertrude Crain has said of her younger son. "Rance, on the other hand, is more interested in editorial ideas and concepts. They make a good team; you need both sets of skills. The support services were moved to Detroit because they [the services] are computerized, and Keith knows how it all works." These services include the corporate financial operation, which was shifted from Chicago to Detroit in 1983, and the Circulation Department, which made the same move in 1985.

Among those brought in by Keith Crain as part of the consolidation of support services in Detroit:

- Jack Lowry, who joined the company as business manager of the Crain Automotive Group in 1982 and became corporate controller at the time of the accounting/financial relocation.

- Robert Adams, who came aboard in 1983 as production manager of *Automotive News* and who later took over as head of the company's production operations, replacing longtime production chief Robert Kraft, who retired in 1986 after 31 years with Crain. Adams now is vice president, production.

- William Morrow, hired in 1985 as senior vice president, "to be responsible for all financial, legal, and administrative operations of Crain and its subsidiaries," Rance and Keith Crain said in a joint statement. In 1990, Morrow became executive vice president, operations.

- William Strong, who had been vice president, circulation, since 1970 and holds that position today, supervised the move of his entire department to Detroit. The circulation department is the largest employer in the company, and maintains its own building in Detroit.

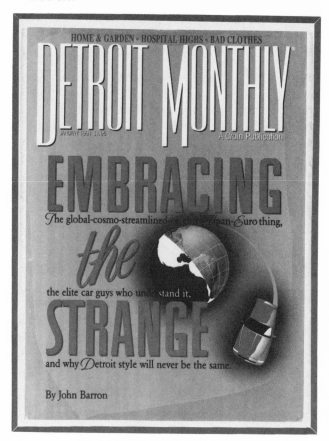

The company ventured into the city magazine field in 1983 with the purchase of *Monthly Detroit*, which became *Detroit Monthly* in 1986, using the slogan: "Now we're literally putting Detroit first."

(Photo by Joseph Wilssens)

With the launch of *Crain's Detroit Business* in February, 1985, publisher Keith Crain (right) watched as Tom Monaghan, president of Domino's Pizza Inc. and owner of the Detroit Tigers, wrote a check for his subscription. Because the pizza chain is known for its free delivery policy, Keith Crain decided to deliver his first subscriber a sample copy of the new publication.

On the editorial side, the company ventured into the city magazine field in 1983 with the purchase of *Monthly Detroit* from its Cleveland owners. The first issue under Crain management appeared in January, 1984. Before the Crain purchase took effect, most of the magazine's staff quit and eventually formed a competitor, *Metropolitan Detroit,* which in 1988 was bought by Crain and folded. (In 1986, *Monthly Detroit* had reversed its names and became *Detroit Monthly,* using in its promotion the phrase "Now we're literally putting Detroit first.")

In February, 1985, *Crain's Detroit Business* was launched, just a month after the birth of *Crain's New York Business.* The new book, with Keith Crain as publisher and Peter Brown (now editor of *Automotive News*) as editor, brought to four the number of weekly business tabloids published by the company.

Keith Crain stressed in his column in the initial issue of *Detroit Business* that the auto industry was well-covered in numerous publi-

AutoWeek, purchased by Crain in 1977, underwent a major overhaul in 1986, with the weekly downsized from a tabloid to standard magazine format. Its paper quality also was upgraded, and the use of color increased.

cations, including *Automotive News,* and that *CDB* would "concentrate on the non-automotive side of business life in the Detroit area, from Pontiac to Flat Rock to Ann Arbor.

"There is a tremendous amount of business news happening in Detroit," he wrote. "Unfortunately, most of it has been unreported." Among topics covered in that first issue: the fierce battle for advertising and readers between the *Detroit Free Press* and the *Detroit News;* the Grand Trunk Western Railroad's request to the federal government for a piece of Consolidated Rail Corp. (Conrail); and the soft sales of Detroit-based Stroh Brewery Co. brands in its home town. These types of stories set the editorial tone for *CDB* as it became established in the Detroit area and edged into the black in its second year. (In 1991, an International edition of *CDB* was launched. Similar in appearance to its parent, this quarterly is given to all first-class and business passengers on international flights from Europe to Detroit. About 30,000 copies were distributed in the first three months of the experiment.)

Automotive News continued its steady circulation growth through the decade, rising from 66,500 in 1980 to more than 79,000 ten years later, although success was punctuated by sadness in 1988 with the death of Robert Lienert at 61. The recently retired editor of *AN* had been with the publication for 34 years and was its editor from 1974 until 1985, when ill health forced him to relinquish that role and become editor-at-large.

AutoWeek underwent a major overhaul that kicked in with its January 1986 issue. The weekly downsized from tabloid to standard magazine format, upgraded its paper to a glossy, coated stock and increased the use of color. And in 1988, *AutoWeek* got a new publisher. Leon Mandel, a 25-year veteran with the magazine and most recently its editor-in-chief, moved into the publisher's chair succeeding Keith Crain, who became editorial director.

In January, 1987, as part of a structural reorganization, the Crain Automotive Group was formally merged into Crain Communications. In a memo to Automotive Group employees, Keith Crain said that "although there has been no difference between the two companies for over a decade, this merger will eliminate any confusion...Rest assured that nothing has changed, as your benefits, profit sharing and pension plans would remain the same. So, welcome to Crain Communications Inc., but you have really been here all the time."

Chapter 16

Action on All Fronts

Through a mixture of business savvy and self-promotion . . . the Crains have more than outstripped the growth of the [specialty-business publishing] industry.
—Wall Street Journal, June 14, 1985

During the 1980s, the growth of Crain Communications attracted the attention of the *Wall Street Journal* and other national publications, and for good reason. Not only in the Motor City, but also across the country, startups, acquisitions, divestitures, and other corporate developments were occurring with mind-spinning frequency throughout the "Reagan Decade."

The company expanded into Florida with the purchase of a quarterly tourism magazine, *Humm's Guide to the Florida Keys* (1982), the monthly *Florida Keys* magazine (1985), and FM station WWUS (1985), broadcasting from Big Pine Key with an adult contemporary format. (The two magazines were sold to Gibbons Publishing in 1990.)

Akron played its part in the expansion as well. In April, 1983, the fortnightly *Tire Business* was introduced, with Ernie Zielasko as editor and publisher. The tabloid newspaper, targeted to independent tire dealers and others involved in the sale and marketing of both new and retreaded tires, did not carry advertising until July, 1984. "One of the reasons we started *Tire Business* is that it was a logical extension of *Rubber & Plastics News*," Zielasko said, "and tire dealers, with few exceptions, weren't getting *R&PN*. Today, *Tire Business*, edited by Ernie's son David Zielasko, has a circulation of slightly more than 20,000, of which about 13,000 is controlled, with the remainder paid.

Tire Business, targeted to independent tire dealers and others involved in selling new and retreated tires, was started in 1983. The tabloid was, said Ernie Zielasko, "a logical extension of *Rubber & Plastics News.*"

Buoyed by the relative early success of its Chicago and Cleveland weeklies, the company took on the biggest business center of them all with the introduction of *Crain's New York Business* in January, 1985, after testing the waters with two "charter issues" in late 1984. And as he did with *Chicago Business,* Rance Crain passed out free copies of *CNYB* to commuters during the rush hour in Midtown Manhattan.

"Our niche in New York, as it has been in Chicago and Cleveland, is to concentrate on second- and third-tier companies," Rance wrote in an early issue. "These often are the companies doing business primarily in the New York area, and they're also the companies too often overlooked by the daily newspapers . . . But the most important ingre-

As he did years earlier with the startup of *Crain's Chicago Business*,
Rance Crain took to the streets of New York to pass out free copies of
Crain's New York Business on its debut in 1985.

dient of our newspaper will be hot news, news that neither the dailies
nor anybody else has dug up."

Gerry Byrne was the first publisher of *CNYB*, and Robert Harris,
who had been *Electronic Media's* first editor, was at the helm during
the early days. When Harris left to become managing editor of the
Journal of Commerce in December 1985, he was succeeded as editor
by Greg David, who had been managing editor and special projects
editor of *Crain's Chicago Business* before he moved to New York to be
CNYB's first executive editor. And in 1987, Byrne shifted to the new
post of vice president/corporate communications, with Gloria Scoby,
associate publisher of *Chicago Business*, becoming *CNYB's* publisher.

As the New York and Detroit business weeklies were making their
debuts, Crain introduced another publication, *City & State*. A spinoff
of *Pensions & Investment Age*, *C&S* actually had appeared three times
during 1984—April, August, and November. But it began publishing
on a regular (10 times a year) schedule with the January-February

1985 issue. At the beginning of 1986, the tabloid became a monthly, and two years later its frequency was increased to fortnightly.

Its purpose, as set forth in early editorials:

> "*C&S* will be edited for elected, appointed, and career officials who manage business and financial affairs for state, city, municipal and county taxpayers, much in the same way scores of business publications are edited for business executives and owners of stock in corporate America" and "the notion behind *City & State* [is] that there is a national communications void of timely information for those who preside over the finances of our cities and states."

Stephen Gilkenson, who had been publisher and editor-in-chief of *Pensions & Investment Age*, moved over to *C&S* with the same titles, and *P&IA* ad director William Bisson moved into the publisher's chair. Michael Clowes, editor of *Pensions & Investment Age*, did double duty by serving as the editor of the new publication in its early stages. The current *C&S* publisher is Dan Miller, the longtime editor of *Crain's Chicago Business*; another *CCB* alumnus, Ellen Shubart is editor. *CCB* managing editor Mark Miller moved up to that paper's editorship when Dan Miller—no relation—became *City & State* publisher.

In 1984, *Advertising Age* introduced both a new editor and a new edition. In April, veteran executive editor Fred Danzig replaced Todd Fandell, the former corporate editor who had been *Ad Age* editor since 1981 and who left the company. Longtime managing editor Lawrence Doherty assumed the new post of deputy editor.

Later that month, *Ad Age* became a twice weekly with the introduction of its Thursday edition, initially an eight-page "wrap" encasing a Magazine section that consisted of the weekly Special Report, features, and columns. A promotional box in the Monday issue preceding the debut said that, "With the torrent of business, marketing, and advertising news steadily increasing, the new Thursday edition becomes the vehicle that enables us to deliver four more pages of news from all corners of the U.S. and [from] correspondents around the world."

Advertising Age Thursday was greeted with uneven reviews. Despite the lively writing and the contemporary graphics in its feature pages, it received little advertising support outside the Special Reports. Some readers praised it, but others complained that two issues a week of *Advertising Age* gave them "too much must reading," a

City & State began publishing on a regular (10 times a year) schedule early in 1985. A spinoff of *Pensions & Investment Age*, it was, in the words of early editorials, "edited for elected, appointed, and career officials who manage business and financial affairs for state, city, municipal, and county taxpayers, much in the same way scores of business publications are edited for business executives and owners of stock in corporate America."

mixed blessing indeed. Over the next two years, the format of the Thursday edition was altered twice, with features, particularly those focusing on the creative process, increasing while the space devoted to breaking news was reduced.

The last issue of *Ad Age Thursday* appeared March 13, 1986, with many of its features—and Special Report—incorporated in the Monday edition. Rance Crain expressed his disappointment in his *Ad Age* column the following week, but he saw some sunshine through the clouds. "*Thursday* introduced a lot of young people to *Ad Age*, and we developed a lot of features we otherwise might not have tried," he wrote. "It helped circulation climb to almost 90,000 from 76,000 in just two years. We're looking forward to serving those 90,000—and more—with our combined Monday issue."

In addition to the features that lived on after *Ad Age Thursday's* demise, another legacy remained: The emphasis on showcasing creative talent and trends. In September 1986, a new "magazine" sprouted and began appearing monthly in New York-area copies of *Ad Age*.

Called *New York Creativity*, it focused on agency creative and art directors, commercial production and music houses, animation and special effects experts, casting agents, and the graphic arts and printing fields.

Later, other editions of *Creativity* were added for the Midwest and California. Today, the slick magazine, with advertising aimed specifically at creatives, is stitched into more than 47,000 copies of *Ad Age*— about half its circulation—on the first Monday of each month.

One of the Crain success stories of the 1980s is *Modern Healthcare*, which grew with the rapidly expanding field it covered. In January, 1988, the magazine went from a fortnightly to a weekly, and by the decade's end, it boasted a total circulation, paid and controlled, of more than 80,000, making it one of the leading publications in the healthcare field. Clark Bell, a veteran newspaperman and former marketing columnist for the *Chicago Sun-Times*, became its editor in 1986, succeeding Donald Johnson, who left the company.

In March 1989, the Akron operation added to its stable with *Plastic News*, a weekly tabloid covering the plastics industry globally, with Chris Chrisman as publisher/editorial director and Robert Grace as editor. An editorial in the first issue stated that existing publications in the field, most of them monthly or less frequent, had done a "commendable job" of covering the activities of the large multinational resin and machinery suppliers, "but they have all but ignored one vital segment of the industry—the product makers.

"These processors, in general, have tended to keep a relatively low profile," the editorial continued. "We want to change that. It doesn't matter whether you are a small custom molder or the plastics division of General Motors or IBM. *Plastics News* is meant to be your publication."

Plastics News quickly proved to be an idea whose time had come. By the end of 1990, its circulation had reached 60,000, of which 10,500 was paid. "We had our first profitable month in June '91," Chrisman said. "And we're shooting for 100% paid circulation by 1996."

Some other benchmarks of Crain publications since the early 1980s:

- *Industrial Marketing*, the oldest continuous Crain periodical still being published, became *Business Marketing* in April 1983, because of the broader definition of the word "business." Bob Donath, then editor and later publisher of *Business Marketing*, wrote that the magazine was increasing its coverage of such fields

Crain's Akron office added *Plastics News* to its roster in March, 1989. By the end of 1990, the weekly tabloid had a circulation of 60,000—10,500 of which was paid. Publisher Chris Chrisman reported that *Plastics News* had its first profitable month in June, 1991, and that it was aiming to have 100% paid circulation by 1996.

as electronics, telecommunications, office automation, and computer-aided design and manufacturing, among others, which are generally termed businesses rather than industries.

- *Business Insurance* marked its 20th anniversary in October, 1987. Publisher Alfred Malecki looked back with justifiable pride, pointing out that *BI's* aggressive journalism had resulted in, among other things, its being the first publication to print insurance details after the Kansas City Hyatt skywalk collapse in 1981 and the only publication to obtain details of the 1984 agreement allotting liability among the makers of Agent Orange.

- *Pensions & Investment Age* in January, 1990, at the urging of William Bisson, reverted to the name it had carried from its inception until 1979—*Pensions & Investments*. The reason for the change, said Editor Mike Clowes in a letter to readers, was that the longer name was simply too cumbersome, and that most people both in-house and outside used the shorter title anyway. At the same time,

P&I reorganized its news hole and added two new features, Front-lines, with short, newsy items increasing the publication's story count, and Commentary, a page on which readers can express opinions on current topics.

- *Advertising Age* marked its 60th anniversary in 1990 with a special section in the June 18 issue featuring a broad-ranging history by Editor Fred Danzig, a reminiscence of the publication's founding by Sid Bernstein and articles on each of the publication's six decades by people who made news in those decades, including Don Ameche, Mary Wells Lawrence and Ralph Nader.

- *Electronic Media* introduced a one-page fax news service in August, 1991. The Daily Fax, distributed from *EM's* Chicago office Tuesday through Friday at 4 P.M. (Eastern Time) includes breaking news as well as ratings information and news of personnel changes.

In 1985, National Textbook Co. (now NTC Publishing Group) of Lincolnwood, Illinois, took over the operation of the Crain Books subsidiary of Crain Communications. Crain Books had been founded in 1973 and published dozens of titles on such advertising and marketing subjects as TV commercial production, market research, cable television, trademark and copyright law, and direct marketing, as well as biographies and memoirs of famous advertising figures. The joint venture with NTC gave books with the Crain imprint wider distribution and the greater editing and marketing resources that an established book publisher can provide.

As the decade of the 1980s rolled to a close, a long-overdue honor was bestowed upon Sid Bernstein: On March 28, 1989, he was inducted into the Advertising Hall of Fame at a ceremony at the Waldorf-Astoria in New York. An *Advertising Age* editorial marked the occasion:

"From the time he started out in business journalism 65 years ago, he has always kept a sharp eye on the advertising business, ready to praise the good, skewer the bad. He has taught us to be true to the values that embody responsibility and progress, and he also challenges advertising to help mankind sustain its ideals."

Chapter 17

The Challenges of Growth

*It's harder now, with the company so big, but I try
to keep abreast of the employees and what's going
on in their lives.*

—Gertrude Crain, 1991

Must a company become more impersonal when it grows larger?
Crain Communications' Board Chairman Gertrude Crain doesn't
think so, although, as the above quote indicates, size tends to bring
complexity, and in recent years, Crain Communications has become a
complex organization indeed.

With 24 publications, a radio station, 1,000-plus employees, extensive computerization in all departments, and offices in New York, Detroit, Chicago, Los Angeles, Dallas, Washington, Cleveland, Akron,
and London, plus correspondents and advertising representatives in
many more cities both in the U.S. and abroad, Crain clearly is big
business. In *Advertising Age's* own rankings of the 100 Largest U.S.
Media Companies for 1990, the company placed 99th, with net revenues of $150.1 million, a 3.4% increase over 1989.

But it is still a closely held private company, and still essentially a
family operation. "I've always had an open door philosophy, just like
my husband did," Gertrude Crain has said. "And running the profit-
sharing and pension plans as I do keeps me close to what's going on."

What's going on is that as Crain has grown—and most of that
growth has come in the last 20 years—so have its ancillary compo-
nents. The organization G.D. Crain knew was basically a three- or
four-publication company with a few dozen employees, most of whom
he knew by name.

Advertising Age, which marked its 60th anniversary in 1990, continues each year to rank the 100 Leading National Advertisers, as well as the largest advertising agencies and media companies.

Whether those were the "good old days" is debatable, but they were, of course, simpler times. Any organization that prints and distributes more than 3.5 million copies of its publications every month, as Crain does, must by necessity have a complex structure. Accounting, circulation, personnel, computer systems, and the management of facilities all have grown steadily in importance.

Chicago-based James Franklin, who was hired in 1974 as director of finance and who eventually became vice president, administration, before leaving the company in 1989, oversaw the growth and development of many of these areas, including the computerization of the accounting and circulation operations and the extensive remodeling in the 1980s of the Chicago offices. The New York and Detroit offices also underwent extensive renovation in the late '80s, and the Akron staff moved to larger, more modern quarters in 1987.

The growth of the Crain personnel operation was underscored in 1984 when Frances Scott was named the company's first personnel director. She had been hired as personnel manager in 1980 on the retirement of Jo Cavaliero.

On the editorial side, in 1985 the company named H.L. Stevenson, longtime United Press International editor-in-chief, as corporate editor, a post previously held by Rance Crain and Todd Fandell. Stevenson was charged, in his words, with "improving the quality of the writing, photography and graphics in the Crain publications; finding ways to utilize information printed in these publications; developing electronic databases; organizing workshops for writers, editors and graphics staff members; and overseeing the libraries and photographers."

One of Stevenson's missions has been to direct the Crain News Service, working with Art Mertz. That service now has from 50 to 100 pages utilizing various types of material from the company's publications, particularly the automotive titles. In 1986, Stevenson assisted James Franklin in reaching an agreement with the Nexis database service, which he said "now brings us more than $200,000 a year in royalties." Stevenson retired late in 1991.

From Gertrude Crain's standpoint, one of the most positive aspects of the company's growth has been that women hold more high positions than at any time previously. "We've always had a lot of women in the company," she said, "but now, they are editors, executive editors, associate publishers and publishers—as they should be."

Currently, four women hold the title of publisher: Gloria Scoby, *Crain's Chicago Business* (who was named in 1989 after having been publisher of *Crain's New York Business*); Alair Townsend, *Crain's New York Business* (1989); Jeanne Towar, *Detroit Monthly* (1990); and Kathryn McIntyre, *Business Insurance,* who succeeded 34-year Crain veteran Alfred Malecki in January, 1992, after 11 years as *BI* editor. McIntyre also has served as *BI's* associate publisher since 1987.

Editors are Ellen Shubart, *City & State* (1989) and Mary Kramer, *Crain's Detroit Business* (1989), who also was named *CDB's* associate publisher in 1990. Nancy Webman has been executive editor of *Pensions & Investments* since 1985. And Penelope (Penny) Geismar, formerly promotion manager of *Automotive News*, was named to the post of corporate communications manager in 1989. In addition, numerous publications have women as executive editors, managing editors, and sales and marketing executives.

Among other major promotions in the late '80s and into the new decade:

- Paul Mitchell, based in London, in 1987 was named managing director/publisher of *European Rubber Journal* and *Urethanes Technology,* the latter a six-times-a-year publication, started in 1984 by Mitchell and Ernie Zielasko, which covers the international polyurethane industry. Mitchell replaced Brian Todd, who left the company.

- Dennis Chase, former *Advertising Age* international editor, in 1987 became *Ad Age's* executive editor, based in Chicago, charged with overseeing day-to-day operations and reporting to editor Fred Danzig in New York.

- William Bisson Jr., publisher of *Pensions & Investments,* Reid Mac-Guidwin, director of marketing for *Automotive News,* and Bob Simmons, publisher of *Rubber & Plastics News* and publications director of the Crain Rubber Group, all became vice presidents in 1988.

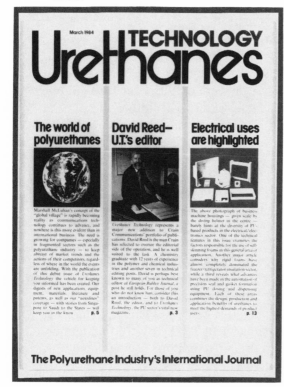

Urethanes Technology, a six-times-a-year magazine based in London and covering the international polyurethane industry, was started in 1984, joining *European Rubber Journal* in Crain's London stable of publications.

- Brian Tucker was named publisher and editorial director of *Crain's Cleveland Business* in 1988. He had been associate publisher and editor. Mark Dodosh succeeded him as editor. In 1990, Tucker was named a vice president.

- Joe Cappo was elevated to group publisher in 1989, overseeing *Advertising Age, Business Marketing, Crain's Chicago Business, Crain's New York Business, Electronic Media, Euromarketing, Pensions & Investment* and *City & State*. (Later in 1989 he also became *Ad Age* publisher, succeeding David Persson, who left the company; Cappo was named senior vice president in 1990).

- Three publishers became vice presidents in 1989: Leon Mandel *(AutoWeek)*, Gloria Scoby *(Crain's Chicago Business)*; and Ron Alridge *(Electronic Media)*.

- Edward Erhardt was named *Ad Age* associate publisher/ad director in 1989, and he became publisher in the fall of 1991, succeeding Cappo, who assumed the title of publishing director.

- J. Clifford Mulcahy, formerly of *Ad Age* sales in New York, became publisher of *Business Marketing* in 1990, succeeding Robert Donath, who left the company.

- Steve Yahn, *CCB's* first editor and the publisher of *Collector-Investor*, rejoined Crain's as editor of *Business Marketing* in 1990.

- James Burcke was named editor of *Business Insurance* effective January 1, 1992, succeeding Kathryn McIntyre, who became publisher of *BI*.

Virtually all of these appointments and promotions exemplify the company's greatest strengths: it's people. From the beginning, Crain has had the philosophy of promoting from within, moving proven performers up through the ranks into key management positions.

As was the case with most other publishing companies, the recession of 1990–91 hit Crain Communications hard, with most of its books posting advertising and/or circulation drops—one notable exception being *Business Insurance*.

Keith Crain has seen some of the ramifications of the economic climate, along with a general trend in publishing. "The pressure [from advertisers] has shifted from the editorial to the business side," he said. "I can't remember the last time we had a serious loss of advertising because of some flap [over a story]. But every day I know of busi-

Business Marketing, the direct descendant of *Class* and *Industrial Marketing*, marked its—and the company's—75th anniversary with this issue in August, 1991.

ness we lose because we won't negotiate rates or sell off the rate card. We don't sell edit, we don't cut rates, and we've never done either.

"Our company has very good reason to be proud of the editorial products we put out. There are no economic influences on our journalists. We have integrity in both editorial and sales."

Just as Keith Crain is committed to the "church-state separation" of editorial and advertising, Rance Crain is committed to continued growth in the company: "I think in the '90s, we'll have opportunities for expansion. There will be more start-ups, and we'll find good, solid acquisitions," Rance said. "We're in a very fortunate position—we have no debt and we're privately held. If we want to take a flier, we can. I don't know of another publishing company with a more solid base to work from.

"My brother and I come to things from a different point of view— that has caused some friction," Rance continued. "But we both want what's best for the company, and we will work in tandem, along the same lines, to continue to push forward."

In 1990, Rance launched a new venture, Turnstile Publishing Co., causing speculation that he might be lessening his involvement in Crain Communications. (Turnstile publishes *GOLFWEEK*, the nation's only weekly golf publication, and *Entertainment Atlanta*, a monthly guide.) "Turnstile is a private investment," he said in response to that speculation. "It does not take my eye off of Crain Communications in the least. Crain will have first refusal for any potential acquisitions that come across my desk."

For Gertrude Crain, like her sons, continued growth remains a high priority—along with warmth.

"I think we're going to be a big company, adding publications that we can handle," she said with a smile. "I don't know that we'll ever get to be a McGraw-Hill, but we'll grow. And I hope we keep the personal touch. I've tried to maintain that touch, and I know the boys will, too."

The Crain Communications board of directors: Front row (from left): Mary Kay Crain, treasurer; Mrs. G.D. Crain Jr., chairman of the board; Merrilee P. Crain, secretary. Back row: Keith Crain, vice chairman; S.R. Bernstein, chairman of the executive committee; Rance Crain, president.

Officers and Directors of
✃ Crain Communications Inc ✄

Directors

Gertrude R. Crain
Sidney R. Bernstein
Rance E. Crain
Keith E. Crain
Mary Kay Crain
Merrilee P. Crain

Officers

Gertrude R. Crain, Chairman
Sidney R. Bernstein, Chairman/Executive Committee
Rance E. Crain, President
Keith E. Crain, Vice-Chairman
Mary Kay Crain, Treasurer/Assistant Secretary
Merrilee P. Crain, Secretary/Assistant Treasurer
William A. Morrow, Executive Vice-President/Operations
Joseph C. Cappo, Senior Vice President/Group Publisher
Robert C. Adams, Vice-President/Corporate Production Director
Ronald W. Alridge, Vice-President/Publisher, *Electronic Media*
William T. Bisson, Vice-President/Publisher, *Pensions & Investments*
Lowell G. Chrisman, Vice-President/Publisher, *Plastics News*
Edwin Goldstein, (Crain Associated Enterprises, Inc), President, *American Trade Magazines*
Charles S. Lauer, Vice-President/Publisher, *Modern Healthcare*
John H. Lowry III, Corporate Controller
M. Reid MacGuidwin, Vice-President/Director of Marketing, *Automotive News*
Alfred Malecki, Vice-President/Publisher, *Business Insurance*
Leon Mandel III, Vice-President/Publisher, *AutoWeek*
Paul Mitchell, (Crain Communications Limited), Managing Director/Publisher, *European Rubber Journal and Urethanes Technology*
Gloria Scoby, Vice-President/Publisher, *Crain's Chicago Business*
Robert S. Simmons, Vice-President/Publisher, *Rubber & Plastics News*
William Strong, Vice-President/Circulation
Brain Tucker, Vice-President/Publisher, *Crain's Cleveland Business*

126

✂ Crain Offices Around the World ✂

Chicago, Illinois
The company's headquarters for corporate activities such as administration, personnel and payroll as well as the headquarters for *Business Marketing, City & State, Crain's Chicago Business, Electronic Media, Modern Healthcare* and *Crain News Service.*
740 Rush St., Chicago, IL 60611-2590.
Telephone: (312) 649-5200.

Detroit, Michigan
Office for corporate accounting and circulation departments, as well as headquarters for *Automotive News, AutoWeek, Crain's Detroit Business, Detroit Monthly, Crain's List Rental Service* and *Crain Computer Services.* 1400 Woodbridge Ave., Detroit, MI 48207-3187.
Telephone: (313) 446-6000.

New York, New York
Eastern editorial and advertising sales staffs of most Crain publications and headquarters for *Advertising Age, Business Insurance, Crain's New York Business* and *Pensions & Investments.* 220 E. 42nd St., New York, NY 10017-5806.
Telephone: (212) 210-0100.

Akron, Ohio
Headquarters of *Plastics News, Rubber & Plastics News* and *Tire Business.* 1725 Merriman Road, Suite 300, Akron, OH 44313-5251.
Telephone (216) 836-9180.

Chicago, (ATM)
Headquarters of *American Trade Magazines.*
500 N. Dearborn St., Chicago, IL 60610-9988.
Telephone: (312) 337-7700.

Cleveland, Ohio
Headquarters of *Crain's Cleveland Business.* 700 West St. Clair Ave.,
Suite 310, Cleveland, OH 44113-1230.
Telephone: (216) 522-1383.

Dallas, Texas
Editorial office. 8950 N. Central Expressway, Suite 114, Dallas, TX 75231-6415. Telephone: (214) 692-9744.

Florida Keys
Offices for *WWUS-104.7 FM,*
Big Pine Key, FL 33043.
Telephone: (305) 872-9100.

Los Angeles, California
Editorial and advertising sales staffs of many Crain publications. 6500 Wilshire Blvd., Suite 2300, Los Angeles, CA 90048-4947.
Telephone: (213) 651-3710.

Nashville, Tennessee
Editorial office. Maryland Farms Office Park, 104 E. Park Drive, Suite 315, Brentwood, TN 37027. Telephone: (615) 371-6654.

Washington, D.C.
Editorial office for Washington editors of various Crain publications. 814 National Press Building, Washington, D.C. 20045-1801.
Telephone: (202) 662-7200.

London, England
Headquarters for *Euromarketing, European Rubber Journal* and *Urethanes Technology.*
Cowcross Court, 77 Cowcross Street, London EC 1 M6BP. Telephone: (44)71-608-1116

Frankfurt, Germany
Editorial office. Justinianstrasse 22,
Lairco-Haus am Holzhausenpark,
6000 Frankfurt am Main 1.
Telephone: (49) 69-59-59-70.

Tokyo, Japan
Editorial office. 7-1 Yuraku-Cho 1-Chome, Chiyoda-Ku, Tokyo 150. Telephone: (81) 3-211-3161.

INDEX